Binnie the Baboon
Anxiety and Stress Activity Book

in the same series

Neon the Ninja Activity Book for Children Who Struggle with Sleep and Nightmares
A Therapeutic Story with Creative Activities for Children Aged 5–10
Dr. Karen Treisman
Illustrated by Sarah Peacock
ISBN 978 1 78592 550 4
eISBN 978 1 78775 002 9
Part of a Therapeutic Treasures Collection

Gilly the Giraffe Self-Esteem Activity Book
A Therapeutic Story with Creative Activities for Children Aged 5–10
Dr. Karen Treisman
Illustrated by Sarah Peacock
ISBN 978 1 78592 552 8
eISBN 978 1 78775 003 6
Part of a Therapeutic Treasures Collection

Presley the Pug Relaxation Activity Book
A Therapeutic Story with Creative Activities about Finding Calm for Children Aged 5–10 Who Worry
Dr. Karen Treisman
Illustrated by Sarah Peacock
ISBN 978 1 78592 553 5
eISBN 978 1 78775 110 1
Part of a Therapeutic Treasures Collection

Cleo the Crocodile Activity Book for Children Who Are Afraid to Get Close
A Therapeutic Story with Creative Activities about Trust, Anger, and Relationships for Children Aged 5–10
Dr. Karen Treisman
Illustrated by Sarah Peacock
ISBN 978 1 78592 551 1
eISBN 978 1 78775 078 4
Part of a Therapeutic Treasures Collection

A Therapeutic Treasure Box for Working with Children and Adolescents with Developmental Trauma
Creative Techniques and Activities
Dr. Karen Treisman
ISBN 978 1 78592 263 3
eISBN 978 1 78450 553 0
Part of a Therapeutic Treasures Collection

A Therapeutic Treasure Deck of Feelings and Sentence Completion Cards
Dr. Karen Treisman
ISBN 978 1 78592 398 2
Part of a Therapeutic Treasures Collection

A Therapeutic Treasure Deck of Grounding, Soothing, Coping and Regulating Cards
Dr. Karen Treisman
ISBN 978 1 78592 529 0
Part of a Therapeutic Treasures Collection

Binnie the Baboon
Anxiety and Stress Activity Book

A Therapeutic Story with Creative and CBT Activities to Help Children Aged 5-10 Who Worry

Dr. Karen Treisman
Illustrated by Sarah Peacock

Jessica Kingsley *Publishers*
London and Philadelphia

First published in 2020
by Jessica Kingsley Publishers
73 Collier Street
London N1 9BE, UK
and
400 Market Street, Suite 400
Philadelphia, PA 19106, USA

www.jkp.com

Copyright © Karen Treisman 2020
Illustrations copyright © Sarah Peacock 2020

All rights reserved. No part of this publication may be reproduced in any material form (including photocopying, storing in any medium by electronic means or transmitting) without the written permission of the copyright owner except in accordance with the provisions of the law or under terms of a licence issued in the UK by the Copyright Licensing Agency Ltd. www.cla.co.uk or in overseas territories by the relevant reproduction rights organisation, for details see www.ifrro.org. Applications for the copyright owner's written permission to reproduce any part of this publication should be addressed to the publisher.

Warning: The doing of an unauthorised act in relation to a copyright work may result in both a civil claim for damages and criminal prosecution.

Library of Congress Cataloging in Publication Data
A CIP catalog record for this book is available from the Library of Congress

British Library Cataloguing in Publication Data
A CIP catalogue record for this book is available from the British Library

ISBN 978 1 78592 554 2
eISBN 978 1 78775 200 9

Printed and bound in Estonia

Contents

About this Workbook — 6
Acknowledgements — 8

The Story of Binnie the Baboon — 9

Activities — 43

    Fun Activities and Crafts to Do with Binnie the Baboon — 44
    Exploring, Understanding, and Learning a Bit More about Worry, Fears, and Anxiety — 53
    Worry Wizard Tricks and Tools — 78
    Some More Important Messages about Anxiety and Worries — 115

Guide for Adults — 139

    Introduction to the workbook and important information about how to use it — 139
    Each child is unique — 140
    What sort of environment works best? — 140
    Who should use this book, what are some of the benefits, and why? — 141
    Not a substitute for therapy — 141
    Structure of the book — 141
    Order of activities and tasks — 142
    Tips about reading this section — 142
    What is anxiety and worry, and what are the key messages about anxiety and worry? — 142
    Understanding a bit more about the processes and thinking patterns which can perpetuate and reinforce the anxiety – a cognitive behavioural therapy cycle — 147
    What are common things that children worry about and fear? — 151
    Questions to expand on understanding the worries/anxiety — 152
    Top tips for responding to worry and anxiety — 154
    Modelling and leading by example — 155
    Naming, labelling, empathising and labelling feelings, and teaching children about their feeling and arousal states — 156
    Mixed and blended feelings – and understanding the child's own experience of that feeling — 159
    Mind-body links — 159
    Externalising and metaphors — 160
    Providing opportunities for mastery — 161
    Consistent and predictable parenting: rules, rituals, and routines — 161
    Some things to be mindful about some of the following strategies, including those in the child's workbook sections — 162

    Coping Tools and Strategies — **164**
    Talking about feeling calm and relaxed — 164
    Safe place exercise — 165
    Creating a soothing and calming box — 166
    What is working well? Reviewing and measuring progress, as well as keeping a record — 168

References and Further Reading — 169

About this Workbook

Hello, my name is Karen. I am a Clinical Psychologist, and I am also the author of this workbook, alongside the creative, friendly, and caring Binnie the Baboon and her jungle friends.

This workbook has helped loads of other children all around the world to make their feelings of worry, fear, stress, and anxiety much smaller. And also, it has helped them to find some calm, some peace, and some sense of relaxation, through using lots of super cool Worry Wizard tricks. You are not alone. This workbook is here to help you to:

- learn and understand a bit more about the things that make the worry, stress, fears, and anxiety visit and get bigger, and how these feelings can impact the way your body and mind feel, the thoughts that you have, the things that you do, and how you feel in different situations and relationships
- learn a bit more about some of the things that make you feel relaxed, happy, and calm, so that these positive feelings can be increased and can outweigh the worrying ones
- find lots of new Worry Wizard tools and ideas for things you can try to do if you are feeling anxious, worried, scared, fearful, and stressed.

What is inside this workbook

- First, there is the illustrated story of Binnie the Baboon and her wonderful jungle friends.
- Second, there are lots of fun activities for you to do around

Binnie the Baboon, such as a colouring-in page, a word search, a quiz, and some special Binnie-inspired arts and crafts ideas.
- Third, there are lots of activities and tips for learning a bit more about worries and anxiety. The more we understand these feelings, the more we can find ways to respond to them, and work with them.
- Fourth, there are loads of different activities, ideas, and tricks on ways to make the anxiety and worry smaller, and ways to help us to feel calmer and more relaxed.
- Then at the end of your sections, there is a certificate from Binnie the Baboon to celebrate you completing and working through this workbook!
- After your sections, there is a whole section for the adult/s who are supporting you with this workbook to read, which gives them lots more ideas, information, and activities to help you. They will read their part *first*, so that they can help you along the way.

Things to remember when reading this workbook

- Take your time — there is no rush. You can do a little bit at a time, and work at a pace that feels right and comfortable for you.
- The adult/s reading the workbook with you are there to help you along the way. Remember you are not alone — as Binnie learns, this is a team effort.
- Different activities and ideas will work and fit differently. We are all unique and special in our own way. No two people are the same. So, you and the adult/s helping you can choose which ideas and activities suit you and which ones you want to try. You know what works best for you!
- The most important bit is that you have fun with it. Be as creative and imaginative as you want! The sky is the limit!

Positive vibes!

From Karen, Binnie the Baboon, and all of their jungle friends!

P.S. You can purchase your very own Binnie the Baboon complete with a zipped tummy with butterflies inside from www.safehandsthinkingminds.co.uk

Acknowledgements

To all the amazing children and families I have worked with who have inspired me so much!

To my phenomenal mum, Binnie (the Baboon), who is the strongest person I know and who is a constant source of love, support, creativity, passion, laughter, joy, resilience, and energy. You are one in a million! Thanks for always being my cheerleader!

To my granny, Ellen (the Elephant), you are so missed and treasured. Your imagination, laughter, optimism, and creativity live on through all of us, and are strongly reflected throughout these books and in the work that I do. Thank you so much.

To Raphy (the Rhino), you will be forever missed and loved. Your infectious laughter, your calming voice, your generous spirit, your deep analysing nature, your wicked sense of humour, your passion and zest for life, your compassion, your empathy, and so much more.

And to my gorgeous nephew, Kace (the Kudu), you are a shining star and bring so much joy, fun, love, pride, and laughter to my life.

To amazing Gabe (the Gorilla), you are a bundle of amazingness, and it has been so exciting watching you grow up and be the fun, smart, adventurous, cheeky, caring, and affectionate boy that you are!

And last, but not least, to Michelle (Michy the Meerkat), my bestest friend, you are the best of the best and I love you to infinity and beyond. Thank you for being you and for your unwavering love, encouragement, thoughtfulness, and support!

I have been so lucky and privileged to have you all in my life!

The Story of Binnie the Baboon

Binnie the Baboon was a colourful, creative, loving, and energetic monkey.

She had big, beautiful eyes, a yellow flower in her furry hair, and she wore a flowing yellow straw skirt. She lived high in the lush green jungle-covered mountains and among the floating clouds of Rwanda in East Africa.

She worried about her family getting sick... She worried about getting wet and cold when it rained... She worried about having nightmares... Binnie worried about EVERYTHING!

Because she was so worried, Binnie was always on high alert – she even jumped when she felt her own skirt tickling her!

Binnie the Baboon even worried about being worried; and if she wasn't worried, she sometimes worried about why she wasn't worried!

When Binnie the Baboon was worried or feeling anxious, different things could happen in her head and in her body.

She could feel very red and hot, as if she was in an oven.

Her muscles could tense up like a soldier stiffly standing to attention, or they did the opposite and went all floppy like wobbly jelly.

Her chest could feel tight as if a weight was being pushed down on it.

Her tummy could feel as if it was doing somersaults or like there were butterflies flying around inside her tummy.

Sometimes her heart could beat very fast – like a thudding drum – and the thoughts in her head whizzed around and around like a whirling tornado.

Binnie the Baboon really didn't like feeling so jittery, so she tried different tricks to get rid of her worries or to make them smaller.

She pushed the worries out of her head to try to stop herself from thinking about them.

She ran away from them by trying to stay super busy.

But this busyness could also make it hard to focus and concentrate, especially when she was at school.

When the worries felt too big, all Binnie could do was think about them, over and over and over again!

At other times, the worries felt so confusing, scary, and big that they came out as big feelings, like anger or sadness.

When the worries felt too big, Binnie the Baboon sometimes thought that the best way to make them go away was to avoid them by not doing the thing that made her feel worried. For example, there was a race through the tallest trees in the jungle. Even though Binnie was a brilliant tree swinger and thought it would be fun, she started to worry...

Will I lose the race? Will I hurt myself? Will the other animals laugh at me?

She had all these doubts. So, in the end, the worries won. Binnie decided not to race and stayed at home while the other animals had fun.

While she was at home, Binnie worried that the animals might think she was silly for not joining in, and felt disappointed in herself for not taking part.

Because of all of these worries and wobbles, Binnie the Baboon often felt that her world was too big, too confusing, and too scary; so, she often felt small, out of control, and full up with thoughts and feelings.

Sometimes, she felt surrounded by the worries and fears, as if she was stuck in a tangled worry web. If only she could get unstuck!

Luckily for Binnie, she had some wonderful friends, teachers, and family members.

There was Michy, who was the most caring and thoughtful meerkat in the whole jungle and was also super at ballet and baking — her scrumptious biscuits were famous throughout the jungle, and she even danced around her jungle kitchen while baking.

There was also Raphy the Rhino. Raphy had a deep, kind, and gruff voice, and an amazing laugh — its sound would echo around the whole jungle and make everybody so happy. Raphy was also funny, mischievous, smart, and a one of a kind rhino. He had a beautiful multi-coloured rhino horn.

There was also Gabe the Gorilla, who was full of energy — he was cheeky, adventurous, and loads of fun! He was also easy to spot due to his piercing green eyes and his green jumpsuit.

Binnie also had her good friend, Chase the Chimp, who was the jungle joker. He loved to play tricks and was also very athletic, so he could do all sorts of swings and gymnastics while he was high up in the tallest trees.

Then there was Kace the Kudu, who was playful, excitable, and smiley. He rocked the entire jungle with his funky trainers and jacket!

Last, but certainly not least, was the graceful, loving, artistic, and warm polka dot scarf-wearing teacher, Ellen the Elephant. She loved painting, teaching, doing crosswords, and going for long adventurous walks.

Michy the Meerkat, Raphy the Rhino, Gabe the Gorilla, Chase the Chimp, Kace the Kudu, and Ellen the Elephant didn't like seeing Binnie the Baboon *so* worried. Michy the Meerkat smiled, 'I know the worries can feel really big and scary, but we're all going to try to help you to learn ways to make them feel smaller and less scary.'

Raphy the Rhino gruffed, 'Binnie, you truly are so much stronger, cooler, and smarter than those pesky worries.'

Gabe the Gorilla chimed in, 'I have a cool idea. You could be your very own Worry Warrior and conquer those jitters!'

Chase the Chimp cheekily chipped in, 'Or you could be a Worry Wizard! Then, you could vanish and shrink those wobbles away!'

Binnie the Baboon sighed, 'I don't feel like a Worry Wizard or a Worry Warrior. I'm scared of my own shadow! I get worried about worrying!'

Michy the Meerkat looked thoughtful, and said softly, 'That's OK, Binnie, everyone has worries. Even roaring lions and fearsome cheetahs have worries. I worry about not doing well in school, like making a mistake or getting told off by the teacher. I also get worried when crossing that rickety bridge — eek — in case I slip down into the crocodile-filled creek.'

Gabe the Gorilla shifted from foot to foot, nodding. 'I might look like the king of the jungle, but I get the wobbles too. I worry about our home staying strong when the storms come, and about not having enough food to eat — and I'm terrified of sneaky spiders!'

Raphy the Rhino rumbled, 'We all have worries. I sometimes worry that I look silly with my colourful horn. I also worry when other animals argue and get upset. And that's just the start of my worry woes!'

Binnie looked shocked. 'I always thought with your tough skin, loud laugh, and spectacular horn, nothing could scare you, Raphy.'

Chase the Chimp chattered excitedly as he swung and jumped back and forth on a nearby tree. 'But do you know what? It isn't all bad. Sometimes worries can actually be really helpful. They can be like our friends and they can give us important messages!'

Binnie the Baboon looked confused. 'My friend? How can worry be my friend? It doesn't feel like my friend!'

Chase the Chimp did a triple flip and landed back on his feet. 'OK, how about when you start to worry about a test at school — it can make you work harder and practise more, then you know you've tried your best! Or if you are worried about getting too much sun, it makes you take shelter and drink lots of water.'

Binnie looked doubtful.

'It can keep you safe too — if you worry about meeting lions on a hunting trip, you might choose to take some strong, brave friends with you — like me — to scare the lions off.' Binnie wavered. 'I guess so.'

Then Binnie started to smile. 'That's true, I suppose. I never thought of the worries like that before.'

Raphy the Rhino croaked, 'So, some worries can be your friend, but others can be pests and can stop you from doing things that you want to do, or from feeling calm and happy — like when they make sleeping harder or make your heart beat fast, or stop you taking part in things like the tree race.

'We need to listen to worries sometimes, but other times we need to find ways to make them smaller or chase them away — if you find you're getting stuck in a worry web, they have too much power and are getting in the way!'

Ellen kindly asked, 'Do the worries sometimes feel as if they follow you around, Binnie, or stick to you like honey?'

Binnie nodded enthusiastically. '*Yes, that's exactly it! So sticky, but not sweet like honey!*'

Gabe rested his giant hand on Binnie's shoulder. 'That sounds awful, Binnie. I am not surprised you are feeling sad. Let's try to find ways to free you from that worry web so that you can do the things you would like to do. I think a Worry Wizard hat would suit you perfectly – and maybe we can add a funky Worry Wizard jumpsuit like mine!'

Chase started to jump up and down on the spot. 'Let's work together as Worry Wizards – after all, lots of heads are better than one, and we have the dream team right here!'

Binnie felt a little shy, but had a happy, warm feeling inside.
'Thanks so much for being such good friends — it means a lot.
So, what should I do now?'

Gabe lumbered forward. 'Well, I can share some tricks I've discovered which have helped me, but you need to find out what works best for you. We're all different! I really like to do relaxation, breathing, and yoga exercises. They help me to slow things down and to keep my cool. When the worries visit, I call them my flutter flies.

'I imagine them flying far far far away from me. Sometimes, I even draw the flutter flies onto a large leaf, and then I watch them floating away along the river, or I huff and puff and blow them away with my strongest breath. HUFF, PUFF, BLOW!'

'At other times, I know it sounds funny, but because the worries can make my body feel really stiff, like a robot, I do lots of stretching and then I shake out the flutter flies to a rhyme.

Shake shake shake them out,

don't you dare even think about hanging about,

move my body to make them fly,

that's how I say a big goodbye.

I'm stronger, bigger, and braver than you are;

now it's time to disappear and fly afar.'

Michy the Meerkat grinned and did her own little shake. 'I like that. I also like music. When I'm feeling nervous, I like to dance or drum to different rhythms. Tap, tap, tappety tap. It really helps me to feel unstuck and to release lots of nervous energy. Actually, so does my baking — all that squeezing the dough and, ooh, those yummy smells!

'I also like to do some breathing; my favourite trick is called hand breathing. It's when you hold out your hand and you trace your fingers. As you trace your fingers, you take a deep breath in through your nose as your travel up the fingers, and then a deep breath out through your mouth when you travel down the fingers.'

Chase piped up, 'I also like to think about all of the things which make me feel happy and calm, including things I like to see, hear, smell, touch, taste, and do. Like lavender to smell, feathers to touch, sunsets to watch, and the chirping of the birds to listen to. These things make me feel calmer, and they make the happy thoughts feel stronger than the worrying ones — they outweigh them!

Raphy the Rhino thoughtfully said, 'I do something similar – it's called being mindful. I look around me and really zoom into things which I can see, hear, feel, and touch – this can help quieten down the noise in my head.

'For example, when I focus on how green or what shape the leaves are, or really notice how they are moving, or the rustling sound they make, or how my feet feel on the ground, or the sun feels on my skin.

'You really have to look around you and soak it in – it's like taking a photo or a film in your mind. Ooh it makes me relaxed just...talking... about...it...zzzz.'

Chase the Chimp gave Raphy a cheeky prod.

Raphy the Rhino awoke with a bellowing chuckle that echoed around the jungle. 'Where was I? Oh yes, well this body doesn't stretch, dance, or shake as well as Gabe or Michy, but when the jitters visit me, I share my worries with others. I talk to people who love me, like all of you.

'I also like to write down my thoughts and feelings, in a diary, a poem, a rap, or a song. Sometimes, so that I have some distance from the worries, I want what I have written down to be far away from me, so I either bury it in the mud, or even better, I have a special place in a tree trunk where I can lock it away — my very own Worry Wardrobe.'

Kace the Kudu chimed in, 'Ooh yes, I like writing too. Sometimes I make my very own Worry Wizard spell to banish those wiggly worry worms. I put all sorts of things into a bowl, like stones, twigs, and feathers, and then mix them with magic words like "abracadabra" and "pow wow"!'

Ellen the Elephant smiled warmly. 'Painting or colouring in is my best way to chase away those wobbles.' Ellen pointed to a pile of stones on the floor. 'Even yesterday I painted stones of hope and happiness, which I can hold when I'm feeling a bit jittery. There is also my poster on that tree of all of the things that make me feel happy and calm.'

Kace the Kudu said, 'Those are all really nice ideas. Another thing that really helps me when I feel jittery is that I think about all of the animals who make me feel loved and protected – my life cheerleaders and my own special team. I imagine them helping me, and outnumbering the worries.'

Chase the Chimp scampered halfway up a nearby tree and hollered, 'Those are cool ideas, but for me, I'm a chatterbox. I talk to the worries and tell them to go away, or to leave me alone. I remind them that I am stronger, cooler, and cleverer than them – and I'm real, not just a worry!

'Sometimes, I climb right to the top of a tree until I'm up in the clouds and look down at the worries. It is amazing how different things can feel and look from a new angle!'

Gabe the Gorilla added, 'I like to remind myself of all of the times I have felt worried in the past, and how I have managed to use all my skills and tricks to get through those times, to the other side. When I started school, I felt super scared, but now I like and look forward to it. Imagine if I wrote all these skills and times down on an "I Can Do It" wall. It would be tall!

'This list also helps me to remember that if I have something new to face, I can take it one step at a time, and that I can do it — and that, sometimes, our minds play tricks on us and it makes the feeling of worry worse than the actual worry itself.

'And sometimes, some of these worries aren't even ours to worry about, which is when we need to try to leave and trust them to someone else, like an adult, whose responsibility they are.'

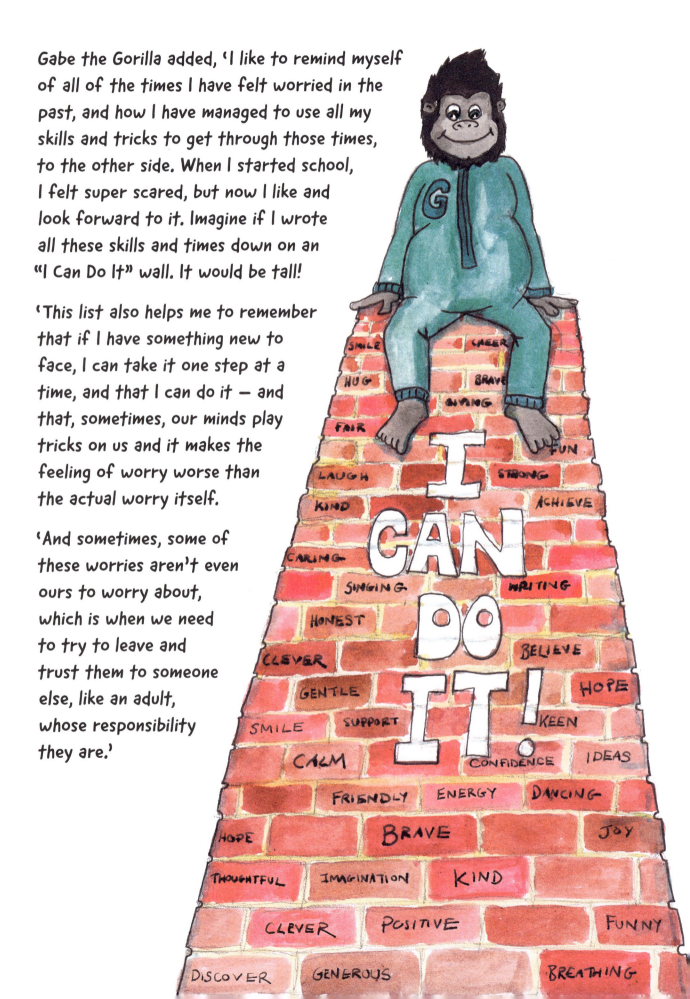

'Wow, that's a lot of ideas! I don't know which to choose and I'm a bit worried about trying, but I will take some time and have a think. I guess if you guys have all found tricks that work, I might be able to as well, or at least I can try,' Binnie said.

Raphy croaked, 'Yes, remember you can be a detective and see what works for you, as everyone is different, and different ones work at different times. You might also have other ideas; these are just a few to get you started. Practise them as much as you can as this really helps. And please be kind to yourself and start small. These things take a bit of time and hope.'

So, over the next few days, with the help of Kace, Ellen, Gabe, Raphy, Chase, and Michy, Binnie the Baboon went about trying a few of the different tricks. They also wrote the tricks down on little cards and on a poster to help her remember, as there were lots to choose from. She tried stretching, shaking, writing, drawing, smelling, breathing, singing, dancing, drumming, talking back, and so much more...

Binnie was surprised, but bit by bit she started to feel as if she did have her very own inner Worry Wizard, and each day it seemed to be growing. Day by day, she was feeling less stuck in a worry web, and the worry wall, which used to tower over her, felt as if it was getting smaller and smaller. She felt as if she was getting bigger and bigger in confidence and wizardry!

The more the worries shrunk, the more Binnie's confidence and hope grew. The drums in her heart felt as if they had slowed down, and the tornado in her head stopped spinning quite so quickly, the oven in her cheeks cooled down, and the soldier in her muscles began to relax. She felt lighter, she could climb higher up in the trees, she could have more fun, she could laugh more, she could sleep better, she could think more, and she even took part in the next tree-climbing race and loved it!

With her new-found confidence, tricks, and tools up her sleeve, a dream team of cheerleaders around her supporting her, her very own inner Worry Wizard, a spring in her step, and a huge smile on her face, Binnie the Baboon danced off into the jungle beaming and bouncing, ready for the adventures which lay ahead.

Activities

Part 1
Fun Activities and Crafts to Do with Binnie the Baboon

Activity 1
Binnie the Baboon Colouring In

Activity 2
Binnie the Baboon Word Search

Can you find all the words listed in the grid below?

```
T G U J X P T C K I E H B O V
W O R R Y Z C M B I Y O I H R
G C U D B R E A T H E J N J C
B D N O I T A X A L E R N S M
D R A Z I W X S E E A C I K S
E E S N Z H E A C A L X E K J
S Y W E I L C D I A A G C L S
T R U Y B T B N T E L I N D J
M A E B A A P A C E R M R U W
A F O T B N V W A T Z E P O J
J W O O T Y X R R D A V S H K
E T O M F U W I P J X N L H I
X N U F U X L Q E I U A E H M
N C G J V W K F Z T X X N E F
Q T H M F B T G S H Y Y E T B
```

ANXIETY   CALM   RELAXATION   WOBBLES
BABOON   FLUTTERS   RWANDA   WORRY
BINNIE   JUNGLE   TRICKS
BREATHE   PRACTICE   WIZARD

Activity 3
Binnie the Baboon Quiz

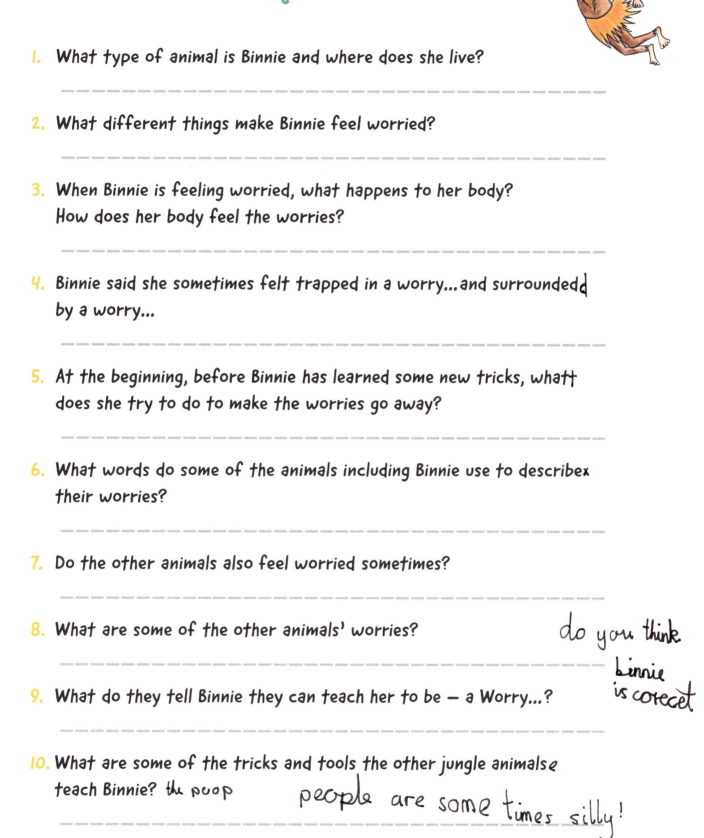

1. What type of animal is Binnie and where does she live?

2. What different things make Binnie feel worried?

3. When Binnie is feeling worried, what happens to her body? How does her body feel the worries?

4. Binnie said she sometimes felt trapped in a worry...and surroundedd by a worry...

5. At the beginning, before Binnie has learned some new tricks, whatt does she try to do to make the worries go away?

6. What words do some of the animals including Binnie use to describex their worries?

7. Do the other animals also feel worried sometimes?

8. What are some of the other animals' worries?

   do you think binnie is corecet

9. What do they tell Binnie they can teach her to be – a Worry...?

10. What are some of the tricks and tools the other jungle animalse teach Binnie? *the poop*   *people are some times silly!*

we did It! ✓✓✓✓ POP

Answers

1. She is a baboon (a type of monkey) and lives in the mountains in Rwanda, which is in East Africa.

2. Binnie worries about what the other animals think about her, and whether they like her. She worries about whether she will fall off the trees or bump her head on one of the branches. She worries about whether she will get lost deep in the jungle, and that she won't be able to find her way home. She worries about what the lurking shadows are that poke out from behind the trees. She worries about her family getting sick. She worries about getting really wet and cold when it rains. She worries about having nightmares. She worries about being worried, or when she isn't worried, she worries about why she isn't worrying, or what she might be forgetting!

3. She feels very red and hot as if she's in an oven – her muscles can tense up like a soldier standing to attention, or they can go all floppy and flimsy like wobbly jelly. Her tummy can feel as if it is doing somersaults, and as if there are butterflies or even busy birds frantically flying around in it. Her chest can feel tight as if a weight is being pushed down on it. Her heart can beat very fast like a banging and thudding drum, and the thoughts in her head can go around and around like a spinning, whizzing, and whirling tornado.

4. Trapped in a worry web and surrounded by a worry wall.

5. She tries to push them out of her head and to stop herself from thinking about them. Or she thinks about them, over and over and over again! Or sometimes she will try to run away from them and to keep super busy, so she will move around and swing really fast to distract her from the worries. Or she tries to avoid them and not do the things that makes her feel worried.

6. Worried, anxious, jittery, wobbles, scared, fear, on edge.

7. Yes, even Raphy the Rhino, Gabe the Gorilla, lions, and cheetahs feel worried.

8. Standing out/the dark/what other animals think/when other animals argue/upsetting other animals/spiders/snakes/school/falling/not having enough food/the weather.

9. A Worry Wizard or a Worry Warrior.

10. There are lots, including: relaxation, breathing, and yoga exercises, like stretching and star breathing. Doing art or music. Shaking it out, drumming, or dancing. Writing it down. Sharing and talking about it with others. Thinking about happy people, things, and places. Playing with, smelling, listening, or looking at things that are happy and calming. Making a magic worry potion. Talking back to the worry. Locking the worry away. Facing the fear, little by little. Thinking about things from another perspective. Remembering all the things that have been overcome in the past and reminding yourself that you can do it and that you are much bigger, stronger, braver, and smarter than the worries.

Activity 4

Some Extra Questions about the Story of Binnie and the Themes Within the Story

Talk with the adult/s supporting you with this workbook about these questions:

1. Who is your favourite character from the story, and why?

2. What is your favourite part of the story, and why?

3. What are some of the things/thoughts/actions that you think make Binnie feel scared and worried? How are these similar to or different from the things that can make you feel worried or scared?

4. What do you think might make Binnie feel happier, safer, calmer, and more relaxed? How are these similar to or different from the things that can make you feel happier, safer, calmer, and more relaxed?

5. What are some of the tricks and tools that Binnie learns about how to calm down and to make the worries smaller? What, if any, calming tricks do you use, or have you seen other people use?

6. What other adventures do you think Binnie might now go on? You could write a follow-up story if you wanted. What would you like Binnie to do?

7. Would you like to have your own Worry Wizard tricks and tools? If so, this workbook is going to help you to find lots of Worry Wizard tricks and tools, but first there are some fun Binnie the Baboon activities for you to do.

Activity 5
Make Your Own Binnie the Baboon - Arts and Crafts

Here are some arts and crafts ideas for making your own Binnie the Baboon (you may also like to make one of her friends).

Paper plate and cardboard Binnie

1. These are two different ways of making a Binnie the Baboon cut-out. Get a piece of card and cut out Binnie's body and head, then colour them in to look like Binnie. Make her arms and legs from four pieces of card, folding them back and forth to look like the elbows and knees. Make her necklace and skirt using feathers, although you can use any material, such as tissue paper, mesh, or straw.

2. The second one is similar but this one uses a paper plate. Cut Binnie's body and face shape out of a paper plate, then draw on her face and body. Use the leftover plate to make her arms and legs and then stick these on.
3. If you prefer you can use the colouring-in image in Activity 1 as a template to trace or to stick onto some card.

Toilet paper and kitchen roll Binnie

1. To make the first creation, take an empty toilet roll and colour in Binnie's body on it. Then draw Binnie's head and feet on a piece of card and add these. If you wish, add a tail made from a pipe cleaner.
2. The second creation uses an empty kitchen roll. Make Binnie as above from paper or card and then glue her onto the

kitchen roll. To add a feeling of movement, make Binnie's arms and legs from card which is folded back and forth. Add leaves, cutting the shapes out of card and sticking the edge of the leaf to the top inner edge of the kitchen roll.

Binnie hand print

1. Draw around or print your hand. Where the thumb is, put a cut-out of Binnie's face.
2. Add her necklace and skirt using card/straw/pipe cleaners, and then draw in, paint, or use materials to make the trees that Binnie is hanging from.

Binnie stress ball

1. You can buy a blank or plain coloured stress ball, or make your own using a balloon and flour/rice.
2. Decorate the stress ball using stickers, felts, paints, or materials.
3. You can put Binnie the Baboon, calming words, calming materials, and so on. Then, each time you squeeze to release the tension, you have Binnie and calming thoughts and words with you cheering you on.

Activity 6
Me and the People in My Life as Animals

Which animal is your favourite, and why? If you were an animal, which one would you be, and why? What would you look like/sound like/do? Where would you live? What different animals would your friends, teachers, and family be, and why?

Draw, sculpt, make, or write your answers below. (Use a different piece of paper if you need more space.)

Part 2
Exploring, Understanding, and Learning a Bit More about Worry, Fears, and Anxiety

Important Messages about Anxiety and Worries

- Having worries and feeling worried is normal. Everyone feels worried at different times, including adults, pets, and superheroes. You are not alone.

- Worry can come in different shapes and sizes, and can last for different amounts of time. There are also lots of different ways we can describe and talk about worry (Activities 7–18 will help you with this).

- Worrying and feelings of anxiety can impact on the way that we think (our thoughts), how our body feels (physical sensations), what feelings we have, and what we do (our behaviours and actions) (see Activities 8–14).

- It is helpful to remember that although worry can come and visit, it will also go away and get smaller. It is like a wave – although it can travel up and feel strong, it will eventually go down. Our bodies are designed to help us make this happen.

- Sometimes, worry is our friend, and it can be useful, as Binnie learned in the story (see Activity 20). For example, it can help us to keep safe, to ask for help, to make us take action.

- Sometimes, we think the best way to stop the worries and to make them smaller is to avoid them, hide from them, and not do the thing that makes us feel worried. Although this often works in the short term, this unfortunately doesn't give us the opportunity to learn that we actually can do the thing that we are worried about, or to practise doing it. This also doesn't give us the chance to learn and discover that sometimes the fear of the fear is worse than the actual fear itself! (See Activities 21 and 41–45.)

- The more we understand how anxiety and worries work, the less scary they will feel, and then the more we can use this understanding to make the worries smaller or go away. This workbook will help you understand them much more.

- Sometimes, our bodies will make us feel that we are in danger when we are not actually in danger, like when a fire alarm goes off over burnt toast – this is still important, but it is not a fire, it is a false alarm. So, this workbook will work with you to learn lots of different ways to calm your body down and to tell it when things are OK, and when it is giving you a false alarm. It will also help you to learn when to listen to your body, like when those worries are your friends and are important.

- It is also important to remember that you are much bigger, stronger, braver, cooler, and smarter than the pesky worries! This workbook is going to teach you how to recognise, celebrate, and remember that, and all of your strengths and inner superpowers – and lots of new tricks and tools – so that you can be your very own Worry Wizard.

Activity 7
Different Choice of Words to Describe Worry and Anxiety

There are lots of different words which people use to describe and name the worries. There is no right or wrong name. Below is a list of some words, and you can circle or colour in which words you use to describe how you feel, or which ones you feel fit best for you.

You might also have your own special name which you can write down in the 'What else?' box. The more we name and describe the feeling, the less scary and overwhelming it becomes.

Worry/ worried	Wobbly/ wibbly	Unsure/ uneasy	Fear/fearful	Stressed
Anxiety/ anxious	Scared	Jelly	Nervous	Afraid
Jitters/ jittery	On edge	Butterflies in tummy	Jumpy	Full up
Flutters	Panicked/ panic	Shaky	Tense	What else?

You may like to use an item, a type of weather, or a thing to describe these feelings instead. The next activity will support you to do this. After that, we will then go on to think a bit more about what the worries are about and how they might make your body and mind feel.

Activity 8
Worry, Fear, and Anxiety Are...

To make the worries and anxiety more understandable and smaller, it can be very helpful to name and describe them. Also, the more we understand the worry, the more we can learn that it is the problem, not us, and that we are much bigger, stronger, cleverer, and cooler than it. Have a look at the pictures below and see if any of them fit for you (there might be more than one, or it might change at different times). Then, with an adult, try to answer the questions which follow. There is also a 'What else?' box where you can make up your own one!

Copyright © Karen Treisman – Binnie the Baboon – 2020

Here are some questions about 'worry/fear/anxiety' (you can replace the words 'worry/anxiety/fear' with your own choice of word — be as creative as you wish). There are lots of questions, so take your time, and feel free to choose which ones fit best for you.

These feelings become much less scary, confusing, and powerful when we understand them a bit more; and when we separate them from ourselves.

- If the worry/fear/anxiety was a colour, it would be...
- If the worry/fear/anxiety was a shape, it would be...
- If the worry/fear/anxiety was an animal, it would be...
- If the worry/fear/anxiety was a flower, a tree, or something from nature, it would be...
- If the worry/fear/anxiety was an object/item/metaphor, it would be...
- If the worry/fear/anxiety could talk, it would say... (What would its voice sound like?)
- I feel the worry/fear/anxiety in my body in my... (see Activities 13–14).
- The worry/fear/anxiety first started visiting me when...
- The worry/fear/anxiety stops me from... (see Activity 21).
- The worry/fear/anxiety helps me and is my friend when... (see Activity 20).
- Without the worry/fear/anxiety, I would...
- If the worry/fear/anxiety disappeared, I would miss...
- ...makes the worry/fear/anxiety much bigger (see Activity 18).
- ...makes the worry/fear/anxiety smaller (see Activity 18).
- A time I felt the worry/fear/anxiety really strongly was when...
- I am stronger and bigger than the worry/fear/anxiety when...
- Any other thoughts/comments...

You can then draw, sculpt, mould, paint, collage, write a poem/story/song/comic about your answers! Some examples follow which other children have done to illustrate their worries.

Scared/Fearful

Worries are like butterflies in my tummy.

Surfing the worry wave.

Feeling weighed down by a worry weight and a worry trap.

Being weighed down by worry stones.

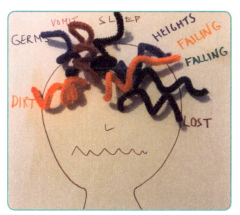

Worries feeling mushy and messy, like having a spaghetti head.

My head full up with too much thought traffic.

The worries piling up on worry tower.

Activity 9
I Worry about

There are lots of different things we can worry about. The pictures below show some common ones (these are just a few ideas so feel free to add some others into the 'What else?' box). Can you please colour in or draw a circle around the thing/s that you worry about, and which make the worry visit you? The more we understand what the worries are, the more we can recognise them and find ways to make them smaller.

Can you share or write some more detail about the one/s which you chose in Activity 9? For example, what is the actual worry? How often do you think about...? Can you think about when it started or why? (Adults, see pages 149–150 for more questions which can be asked here.)

If you chose more than one, which one would you say is your biggest worry, the one which you feel causes you the most problems, the one which if you had a magic wand you would vanish away or try to shrink first?

Now that we have learned a bit more about the worry, the activities on the next few pages help you to think a bit more about them, and creatively show them. There is a worry wall, a worry web, and a worry head. You might like to just pick and fill out one, or you might like to do them all, or instead, you might like to make up your own — whatever you prefer! After the Activity worksheets, there are some photos of how you can take these ideas and make them even more creative and fun!

Activity 10
Worry Web

Many of us, like Binnie the Baboon, can get caught in a web of worries! They can get us in a spin, knot around us, and make us feel stuck or trapped. Using Activity 9, write down or draw on the worry web the different worries and feelings you have. If you want to, you can choose different colours, sizes, and shapes to express the different worries.

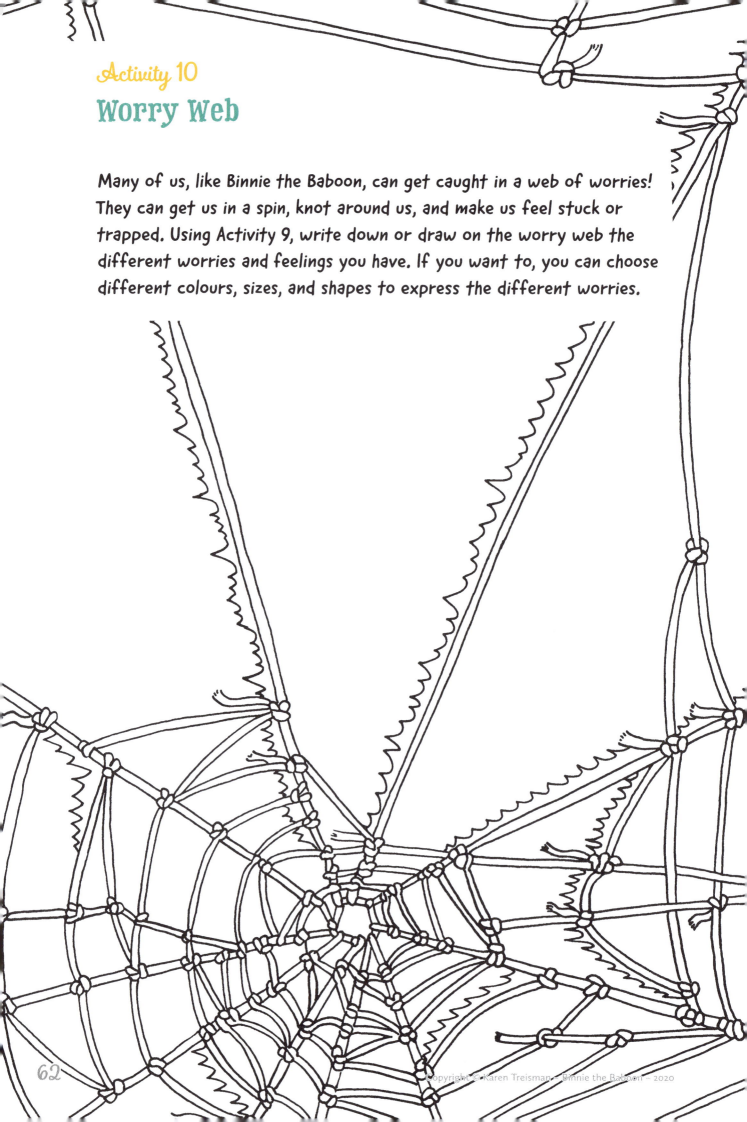

Activity 11
Worry Wall

Using Activity 10, can you please write down or draw, in the different bricks on the worry wall, the different worries and feelings which you have. If you want to, you can choose different colours, sizes, and shapes to express them. As in the photo, you might also like to build your own worry wall using blocks and use labels to write down the different worries and feelings.

Activity 12
Thoughts and Feelings Head

You might also like to write down or draw the different thoughts and feelings which you have on the below head.

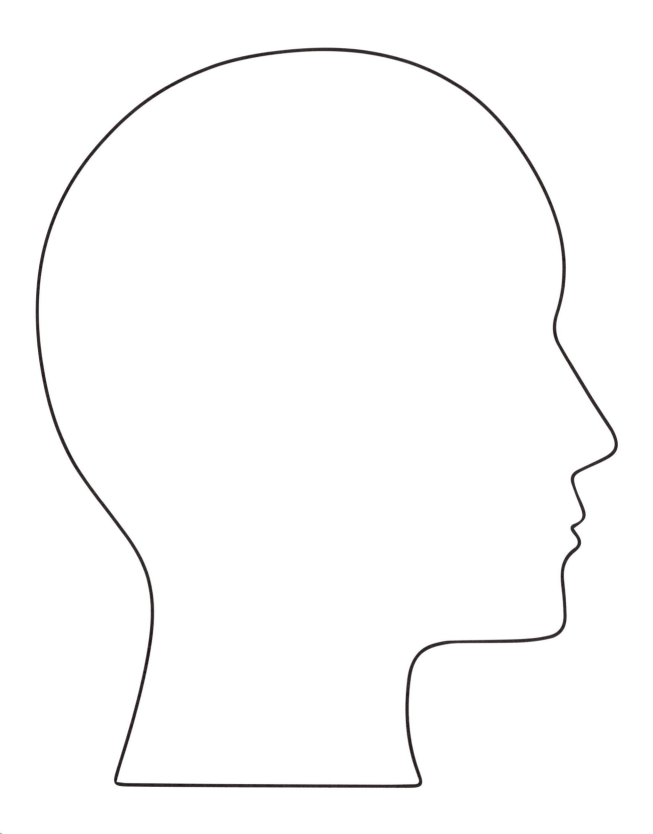

Here are some photos of ideas for taking some of the above activities of a worry head, a worry wall, and a worry web and turning them into a more expressive piece of art or a creation — be as creative as you wish!

Worries in my head using speech marks.

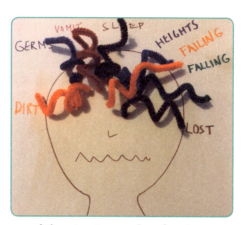
Worries in my head using pipe cleaners.

My worry wall using post-it notes.

Worries on my head using a 3D head and labels.

My worries shown as a worry wall using jenga/building blocks.

Thought traffic in my head.

My worries trapped in my head like a worry web, using wooden sticks and pipe cleaners (you could use things like lollipop sticks, twigs, string, and ribbon as well).

Activity 13
Worries and Anxiety in Our Body

Worries, fears, stressors, tension, and anxieties often are felt strongly in our bodies. It is helpful to learn to recognise and notice these feelings and sensations. This means that we can notice and catch the warning signs and body flags early, and then do something about them. Also, the more we understand something, the less scary and overwhelming it can feel. Can you draw, colour, or write on the below body outlines using shapes, words, or colours?

- Where and how do you feel worry/wobbles/nervousness/fear?
- Where and how do you feel calm/relaxation in your body?
- Where and how do you feel excitement/happiness in your body?
- If your body could talk when it has those feelings, what might it say?

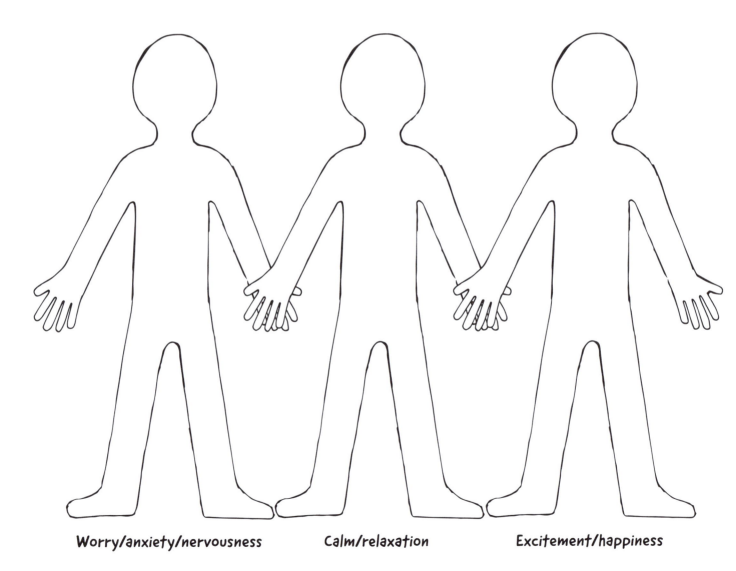

Worry/anxiety/nervousness   Calm/relaxation   Excitement/happiness

Activity 14
Common Feelings, Signs, and Sensations in Our Bodies when We Feel Worried, Scared, Fearful, or Anxious

Worry and anxiety can show itself in our bodies in lots of different ways. Below are some of the common ways bodies can feel when we are anxious. Which ones, if any, do you feel? You can circle or colour these in, or, if you prefer, you can photocopy this activity, cut the words out, and stick them onto a body cut-out, a body outline, or a body doll.

How would you describe these feelings? Binnie felt that her heart beat like a thudding drum, her muscles tensed like a soldier, her chest tightened as if weights were on it, and so forth.

Sometimes, when we hear, think, feel, or see something scary, like a snake or a shark, our bodies are really smart and cool, they spring into action, and they get us ready and prepare us to do something. This might be to stay very still and to hope that we go unnoticed (freeze mode), or to run away, to try to escape (flight mode), or to defend ourselves by fighting back (fight mode). This means that our bodies produce chemicals, called adrenaline and cortisol, which help us to do things like breathe faster, get our muscles ready, and make our heart beat quicker. This is super cool as it gets our bodies ready for action, but the problem is that sometimes our mind and body trick us and send us false or exaggerated signals to get ready when we don't actually need to – like a fire alarm that gets triggered by some burnt toast. So, it is helpful to learn to recognise when the threat is real, and when it is a false alarm, and then we can find ways to tell our body that it is OK.

Trembling/ shaking	Dry mouth/ feeling thirsty	Feeling on edge/ restless/ fidgety/ pacing	Body feeling heavy and weighted down	Nausea and feeling sick
Tense/ stiff/achy muscles/pins and needles/ tingling	Grinding teeth	Talking very quickly/ racing mind/ whirling thoughts/ struggling to speak	Blurred vision	Stuttering and stammering
Heart beating faster/ racing heart	Sweating/ feeling hot and/or red	Rashes or skin irritation	Feeling cold/ frozen/stuck	Change in sleep/ struggling to sleep/ sleeping too much
Floppy/ flimsy/like jelly/shaky	A feeling of dread/panic	Tight chest/ struggling to breathe/ breathing fast/ shortness of breath	Change in appetite, e.g. hungry/not hungry	Needing to go to the toilet/being constipated
Weak/dizzy/ faint/light-headed/ spinning head	Headaches/ heavy head	Fuzzy head/ difficult to think, concentrate, or pay attention	Stomach ache/ butterflies in tummy/ running tummy/ knots in tummy	What else?

Activity 15
Triggers and Warning Signs

To help us learn how to make the worries, anxieties, and fears smaller, and to catch them as early as possible, we need to first try to learn how to recognise the signs, triggers, and clues for when those feelings visit us. This is a bit like being a detective. We need to pay attention and notice. It can be helpful to keep a diary so that we don't forget. To start to help you to notice these things, complete the sentences below about the things which make the worry visit/start/worsen. (Use a large piece of paper if you prefer or make one of the pieces of art that follow.)

1. People that make the worry visit...

2. Places, sights, objects, and/or things that I can see or look at that make the worry visit...

3. Situations that make the worry visit...

4. Smells/tastes/sounds that make the worry visit...

_____

_____

_____

_____

5. Body feelings and sensations that make the worry visit...

_____

_____

_____

_____

6. Actions, words, or things people or I do or say that make the worry visit...

_____

_____

_____

_____

Activity 16
Things that Bug Me

You might like to write or draw some of these triggers and hotspots below — what things bug you, or get under your skin?

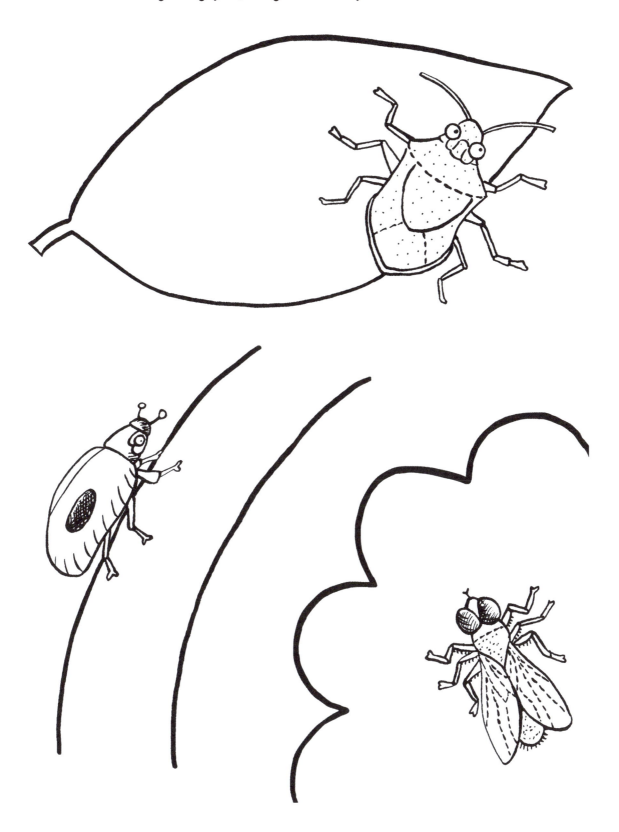

Activity 17
More Triggers and Warning Signs

Building on the above, you might like to draw or represent the triggers and warning signs which you have identified in Activities 15 and 16 in a more creative way. Here are some ideas, but you might have your own too!

Using bug puppets and toys to talk about what bugs you.

Using buttons and remote controls to talk about what things push your buttons!

Using folder paper and drawings to talk about your storm starters or your bolts of lightning.

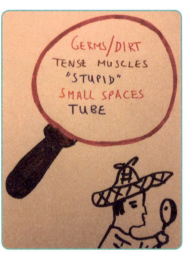

A drawing of a detective looking for different triggers — you could use an actual magnet or net.

Activity 18
What Makes the Worries Bigger or Smaller?

Draw, sculpt, or write down what things make the worries bigger, stronger, and visit more often. Then draw or write down the things that can make the worries smaller, weaker, and stay away. It might include your thoughts, how you feel, what you do, or things that other people do or say. Try to think of specific examples, and about what actually happens during these times.

Bigger and visit more	Smaller and stay away

Activity 19
Before, During, After Diary

Can you think of a specific time when the worry or anxiety visited you? What happened before, during, and after (this might include what happened in your body, in your face, in your thoughts, in your feelings, and in what you and others did)? What did you learn from these times? Are there any patterns which you can see? (Photocopy the table below for additional space and copies.)

The event (Where and when?)	Before (My and others' feelings, thoughts, body sensations, actions, words, etc.)	During (My and others' feelings, thoughts, body sensations, actions, words, etc.)	After (My and others' feelings, thoughts, body sensations, actions, words, etc.)

You might prefer to talk about the before, during, and after using something more interactive like dominos, a paper chain, or a series of thoughts (see photos below) and feelings heads (see Activity 12).

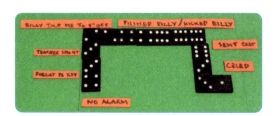

Activity 20
Worry Can Be Our Friend

As we learned in the story of Binnie, worry can sometimes also be our friend and it can have some advantages and important messages. The difficulty is when the worry becomes too big or feels too powerful, or when it gives us false alarms. Write down a list or draw in the box when the worries have or might be your friend and useful to you.

This can be a new way of thinking, so to get you started, here are some ideas...

- Worrying about who to trust might make us cautious around strangers.
- Worrying might give us a clue to let us know that we really care about something.
- Worrying and caring about schoolwork might make us try our best.
- Worrying about getting burnt might make us put on sun cream.
- Worrying about being healthy might make us do things like eat our fruit and vegetables.
- Worrying about having shiny teeth might make us brush them more regularly.
- Worrying about upsetting someone might make us be kinder to others and think before we speak or do something.
- Worrying about something breaking might make us look after it more carefully.
- Worrying about something and feeling unsure might make us ask for help, and help us learn new ways of understanding things and coping with them.
- Worrying about our safety might make us do things like look carefully before crossing the road.

What else? When is worry your friend or useful or helpful to you?

Activity 21
Both Sides of the Worry Wall

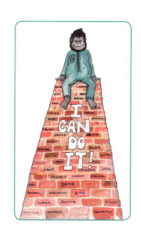

While worries can be our friends, they also can be annoying and can get in our way. They can follow us around like a shadow! When they do this, they can make things which we want to do feel harder or not possible.

- What do the worries stop you from doing/achieving/feeling?
- What do you wish you could do if the worries were smaller and got out of your way?
- If you had a magic wand and could make the worries go away, or to shrink, what would be different?

Write down or draw your answers. So, for example, what is on the other side of the wall which you would like to get to/achieve/do/be easier/feel (e.g. to sleep better, to make new friends, to feel calmer, etc.)? You might prefer to do this on a separate page with a different metaphor, like getting unstuck from the worry web, shrinking the worries with your inner Worry Wizard (Activities 46 and 52), or getting free from worry weights.

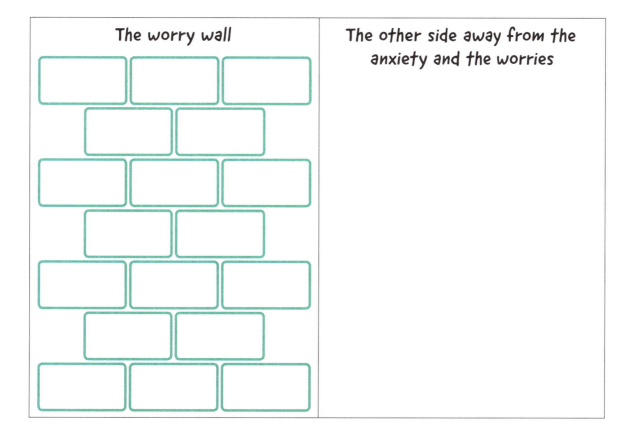

The worry wall	The other side away from the anxiety and the worries

Part 3
Worry Wizard Tricks and Tools

Introduction

We have learned a lot more about the worries and anxiety, including different names for them, what they look like, what makes them smaller and bigger, when they visit, where we feel them, when they are our friend, what they stop us from doing, and much more. Now, like Binnie, we can go on to learn even more tricks and tools to make the worries smaller and feel more manageable. These will help you to be your very own Worry Wizard!

Please remember that everyone is different and there is no right or wrong way. Alongside the adult/s helping you with this workbook, you just need to be detectives and find what works best for you. There might be just one trick which you like, or there might be loads! You might also have your own ideas, so please be as creative as you like, because you know yourself and what works best for you!

So, take your time, try them out, and practise! This makes it so much easier to remember when we actually really need it. It is like taking our brain and our body to the tricks gym!

Lots of different tricks and tools will be described in the following sections, as there is something for everyone. First, there is a section on different ways to express the worries using techniques from something called externalisation – this is where we learn that the worry is the problem, not us. It helps to separate us from the problem, to give us some distance from it, and to conquer it.

Then we will go on to learn some breathing, yoga, and relaxation exercises. Following this, we have some ideas for making the worries smaller, inspired by nature, music, art, and games.

After that, there are tricks about how to make the happy thoughts and memories outweigh the worry thoughts and memories, and how to find a special calm and happy place in our minds, like going to a mind spa or having a brain break.

Then we learn about how we can use our different senses to bring us some calm, and you will have the chance to make your very own calming worry-free box. We will also have the opportunity to make a worry potion!

We will then go on to learn a bit about facing our fears, talking back to them, catching our worries when they trick us into thinking traps, and how to break the thoughts, feelings, and behaviours cycle!

This section will end with remembering all of your skills, strengths, and the things you have coped with before, and all of the people who are around you supporting you.

Then you will be able to escape the worry maze and receive your certificate!

So, let's start strengthening your Worry Wizard!

Activity 22

Creative Worry Wizards Tricks and Ideas for Putting Some Distance Between You and the Worries

Externalising tools

It can be super helpful to write down, draw, make, sculpt, or collage the worries/anxiety/fears and then to find a way to look at them from a distance. This helps to see them as separate to you — they are the problem, not you. When you do this, then you can see the worries, and put words to them, which helps you to see how much bigger, stronger, cleverer, more real, cooler, and braver you are compared to them! This is also helpful as once they are out of your head and on a piece of paper or a piece of art, you can think about them a bit more, see them more clearly, and feel more in control of them. Then, if you want, you can get rid of them, shrink them, or lock them away. Here are some ways which can help you to do this.

- Make or buy a worry box/bag/jar. This is where you draw or write down your worries and put them away or keep them locked away in the box/bag/jar. You can also decorate the outside of the container with feel-good and worry-free messages.

 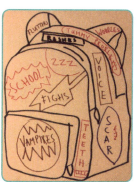

- Write down your worries, thoughts, and feelings in a diary, song, poem, comic, in a story, letter, play, or rap. You can even make a worry postbox or letterbox if you wanted to.

- Write down or draw your worries and release them or let them go! Put them in a message in a bottle which you release on the water, in a balloon that you let float away, on toilet paper which you flush down the toilet, or on butterflies which you can imagine flying away (Activity 23).

- Lock away your worries or feed them to a worry monster, a worry eater, a worry ninja, a worry fairy, a worry wizard, or worry dolls. You can buy these (see www.safehandsthinkingminds.co.uk). They can keep the worries and fears away from you! Or if you prefer you can give them your hopes and wishes to keep close by and safe!

  Or you can make your own worry monster or eater using household items like a cereal box, socks, pipe cleaners, toilet rolls. There are loads of ideas for doing this online.

  Some questions to think about might be (the dots are where you can put the creature's name):
    - 'What is your worry monster's name?'
    - 'What does...look like/sound like/smell like/say/do?'
    - 'What is...'s job?'
    - 'What special powers does...have?'
    - 'How does...protect you?'
    - 'How does...make you feel?'
    - 'How does...gobble up/scare away/crush/squeeze/eat/jump on/catch the worries?'
    - 'How does...keep the positive and happy thoughts safe?'
    - 'How much safer and calmer do you feel knowing that... is with you?'

- You could also make a worry stone, a worry friend, or a worry animal. There are lots of different ways you could use this. For example, you could:
    - give your worries to the...
    - tell them your worries and ask for their support and advice
    - write your worries on them and then get rid of them and lessen your load
    - decorate them with positive and helpful messages which you hold for strength, to ground you, and to look at for inspiration.

- Worry plaques/keyrings. The worry plaque and keyrings shown in the photos are from the Irish Fairy Door Company, and you can give your worries to the worry fairies; the light changes when you put your hand/finger on them and share your worries, and they take them away for you.

- You might like to make some jewellery, with each bead representing a person, a skill, a coping tool, or the things that protect and help you with the worries/anxiety. For example, a bead for my bravery, a bead for my grandma, a bead for my breathing techniques.

- Which is your favourite? Which, if any, would you like to try? Do you have any other ideas? Or are you doing any of these things already?

Activity 23
Flutter Flies

Worries can sometimes feel like fluttering in our tummies. Draw, write, or colour some of your different worries, thoughts, or feelings on the butterflies, or flutter flies. Then you can draw, act, imagine, or sculpt the worries and the flutters flying far far away! What does this feel like?

Activity 24
Relaxation, Mindfulness, Yoga, and Breathing Exercises

Wow, your Worry Wizard hat is growing by the minute! Now that we have looked at some things we can do around writing down and drawing our worries, let's look at some cool breathing, relaxation, and yoga ideas. Remember these were some of Binnie's, Gabe's, Raphy's, Ellen's, Kace's, Chase's, and Michy's favourite ones!

Sometimes, when we want to feel calmer and more relaxed, it can be really helpful to do some calming breathing, relaxation, and mindfulness exercises. Binnie and her jungle friends shared about how helpful these were for them. These exercises can give us a brain and body break, like going to a spa. There are lots of different ideas, but here are some which you can try out, and then afterwards, you can choose your favourite one/s. Take your time as you go through them, and see if you can try them out, and practise them (with the help of an adult). I've also designed a pack of cards for grounding, soothing, coping, and regulating activities which you can purchase to give you plenty more ideas (*A Therapeutic Treasure Deck of Grounding, Soothing, Coping and Regulating Cards*).

Breathing

It is really helpful to learn how to take deep, slow and intentional breaths – these can refuel you, give you something else to focus on, and slow down some of the noise which can be in your head. Here are some fun ways of doing this (start small and choose one to try out first).

Imagine that you are breathing deeply in before getting ready to blow up a balloon, and then exhaling and blowing deeply lots of air into the balloon to fill it and blow it up. Try breathing in while thinking about all

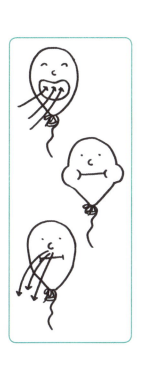

of the good and happy things in your life, and then breathe out all of the bad, worrying, upsetting things. Instead of a balloon, you might like to pretend that you are like a train, blowing steam, or that you are blowing out birthday candles, or thistles on a dandelion!

Michy the Meerkat used hand breathing. You can do this too! Try holding out your hand. Trace and move the finger around your hand and breathe in through your mouth each time you move upwards along a finger; then breathe out through your nose each time you move back down again. You can also swap around, and breathe in through your nose and out through your mouth (see Activity 25).

You can also do the above breathing with lots of different shapes, for example around a hexagon, a square, and a star, going up and down, breathing in and out as you follow the shape.

 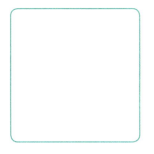 

Choose a relaxing, soothing, calming, and warm colour, shape, or sound (you can choose more than one if you prefer). Breathe in and imagine that that colour, shape, or sound is travelling gently through and around your body – from your feet to your head and spreading all around.

Another trick to help with breathing is to rest a soft toy on your tummy and then slowly breathe in and then out. Watch the toy rising and falling with each breath.

You might also like to make your very own mindful magic wand or breathing creature by taking a toilet roll/kitchen roll, decorating it, and then sticking some colourful strips of tissue paper inside it. This can then be used to blow into, and to practise your deep breathing.

Take a moment and try one or more of these. Which ones do you like? What do you notice?

Stretching and moving

One way to relax is to stretch and move your body around. Here are some of my favourite ways of doing this.

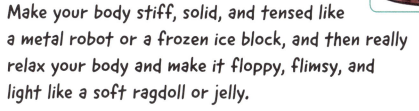

Make yourself teeny tiny, like a curled-up mouse or a snail, and then stretch to be really high and tall like a giraffe or a tree.

Make your body stiff, solid, and tensed like a metal robot or a frozen ice block, and then really relax your body and make it floppy, flimsy, and light like a soft ragdoll or jelly.

Make yourself wriggle around like a caterpillar, and then grow and change into a butterfly with outspread wings.

Practise stretching your whole body – go through each body part in order, and tense and relax each of your muscles: your feet, calves, tummy, shoulders, arms, fists, teeth, face, and so on. So, for example, with your fists, you would tense them and squeeze them really tightly like a boxer; and then really open up and stretch them out and relax your hands. Try to do this two to three times.

Try standing very straight and stiff, and then really shaking and wobbling and jiggling your body around.

You might want to find a movement that helps you to feel calm and soothed. Some common ones are crawling, hanging, rocking, balancing.

You might want to use a stress ball or a squishy ball to squeeze and release. To make this work even more, try to change which hand you hold the stress ball in; for example, left then right, left then right. You can buy a stress ball, or you can make your own using a balloon and some beans/rice/flour. Another great addition is to get your own stress ball and decorate it with positive and calming pictures/words/stickers.

You might also like to try some soothing, fun, and stretching yoga poses as seen here:

Take a moment and try one or more of these. Which ones do you like? What do you notice?

Guided imagery

Guided imagery is a super cool mind-body technique that can help you to relax your mind and body. This is where we can travel to a happy thought, moment, and feeling in our minds — like a mind retreat or a head spa. Everyone will have different ones which they like, so here are just a few ideas to get you started. Imagine that you are:

- floating on a cloud
- riding on the back of a unicorn or horse
- drifting in a hot air balloon
- swimming with dolphins
- walking on a beach
- being hugged by a tree
- wrapped in a warm snuggly blanket
- flying and gliding through the air
- floating in warm water/the sea
- walking through a secret garden or an enchanted forest
- watching the sun rise or set.

It can also help once you choose one of these to have a reminder, for example for the beach one, holding a shell, looking at a picture of a beach, or listening to the sound of the ocean.

Take a moment and try one or more of these. Which ones do you like? What do you notice?

Mindfulness

Mindfulness sounds complicated and like a big word, but it's a simple technique that involves trying to be still and quiet and think about what's going on for you and in your world in the present moment — thinking about your feelings, how your body feels, and what your thoughts are. This can help you to really notice and take in your environment, and your surroundings. Being mindful involves focusing on all of your different senses. It's like being a superhero with zooming-in vision — what can you smell, hear, see, taste, and touch around you?

For example, if you go out on a walk, try to notice the leaves on your journey. Are there a lot of them? What colours, shapes, and sizes are they? Feel their texture, listen to the sound they make when you tread on them, and watch how they float down from trees and rustle in the wind.

You might also want to look around you when you are in a room and really pay attention and zoom in to what you can feel, see, hear, notice, and touch. You can also set yourself a list – for example, can you look for something soft, look for something that is brown, look for something that is round? It is a bit like playing I Spy (see Activity 26).

You might also want to fill a box with pompoms or cotton wool balls. Slowly count how many there are, and then calmly take each one out, breathe deeply in and out, notice and look at it – what is its shape, what colour is it, how does it feel? This is sometimes called a calm counting box.

Take a moment and try one or more of these. Which ones do you like? What do you notice?

Activity 25
Hand Breathing

Michy the Meerkat used hand breathing. You can do this too! Try holding out your hand/s. Trace and move the finger around your hand and breathe in through your mouth each time you move upwards along a finger, then out through your nose each time you move back down again. You can also swap around, and breathe in through your nose, and out through your mouth.

Activity 26
Grounding and Mindfulness

Look around you. Name and describe at least one, but preferably three, things that you... (If you can't, you can imagine something you would like to, for example, see.)

👁 **See...**
_____
_____

👂 **Hear...**
_____
_____

👃 **Smell...**
_____
_____

✋ **Feel...**
_____
_____

👅 **Taste...**
_____
_____

As you are doing this, really zoom in, notice, soak it in, and breathe slowly and gently.

Activity 27
Nature, Music, Art, and Cognitive Games

Binnie and her jungle friends have even more coping tools and activities which you could try (remember, everyone is different).

Nature

Spending time in nature can be really fun, calming, and relaxing. This could mean just going for a walk, going for a bike ride, playing outside, going vegetable or fruit picking, gardening, going horse riding, or doing some sports, but remember to make this time even more calming. Really try to notice and pay attention to your senses — what you see, hear, feel, smell, and taste. You might even like to play I Spy using all these things in nature. There are also some other activities (just a few ideas) which you could do to take nature to a whole new level!

- Trace or paint leaves, cones, stones, trees, and much more. You could even turn these into a leaf mobile or person (as in the photo).
- Make stamps or stencils from nature.
- Take photos or collect different pieces and then make a nature collage or scrapbook.
- Make a word or a name acronym using different pieces from nature (as in the photo).
- Make a nature treasure basket (as in the photo).
- Have a nature scavenger hunt. This is where you look for certain things outside in nature — for example, can you find something green, can you find something round, can you find something soft?
- Make an obstacle course around the different things in nature, like doing star jumps round the big tree, or doing hops to a bench.
- Collect flowers and make nice smelling perfume or a magic potion.

Music

Music can also be a great way to help us release, feel, and express ourselves, our feelings, our story, our thoughts, and our sensations.

Choose a favourite song that you can listen to, hum to, or can sing, one that makes you feel happy, calm, and relaxed.

You could also dance, shake-it out, or write down the words to the song. You could also play an instrument or even make your own instruments to play!

Using rhythm can also be lots of fun and can really change our mood. You and the adults around you can copy or make up rhythms to clap, tap, stamp, or drum to!

My favourite and feel-good songs are…

My favourite song to cry to and release my feelings is…

My favourite singer/band is…

If there was a song to show how I was feeling today, or about… it would be…

Arts and crafts

Doing arts and crafts and being creative is another great way we can express, release, feel, and explore things. It can also help us to use different parts of our brain and body, and can keep us focused on what we are doing, rather than the thoughts that buzz around in our mind.

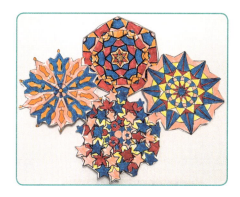

There are no limits to the type of art you can do – the possibilities are endless, but here are some ideas:

- Colouring in, drawing, or painting.
- Sticking stickers.
- Ripping papers up and/or making collages, a scrapbook, decoupage, or papier mache.
- Making visual journals and diaries.
- Making paint blots (where you splat paint on a piece of paper, fold the paper, open it up, and see what shapes you have made).
- Sculpting, moulding, or making a three-dimensional item.
- Sewing, knitting, or other needle work.
- Decorating an item like candle painting, glass painting, or painting a jewellery box.
- Jewellery making.
- Pipe cleaner art.
- Mandala colouring in and making.
- A lovely addition to this is making a paint splotch or a random mark and then turning it into something pretty. This is great to learn that a 'mistake', an 'oops', can be fab too!

Cognitive games

Sometimes cognitive games can be a good distraction, and they can help us focus on something else. This might be things like:

- Can you think of animals, activities, types of foods, names, countries with the letter…?

- Playing I Spy.
- Playing I went shopping and I bought…
- If I ruled the world I would…
- If I could do anything right now I would…
- Doing a puzzle, a Rubik's cube, a maze, a crossword, memory/matching games, or playing a game like Sudoku or Scrabble.

Another great thing to try is to have some allocated 'worry time'. This is some time set aside every day or week where you can think, write down, share, and express as much about your worries as you like. But then once you have finished, you close the door on the worry time, and move on to another activity.

Also, it can be very helpful for some people to write down a list of things to do, and then to visually cross off or delete the things which they have completed.

We have learned lots of different relaxation and creative Worry Wizard tricks. We are now going to go on to learn even more tricks. Goodness, that Worry Wizard hat is going to be huge! We are going to look at ways to make the happy thoughts grow bigger and outweigh the worries. We will also learn how to find a special happy and calming place, and how to make our very own calming and relaxing box!

To help you to do this we need to learn a bit more about what calmness, relaxation, and safety feel like and mean to you, in Activities 28–30.

Let's go…

Activity 28
Happy, Calming, Relaxing, and Positive Thoughts

Often, we need to try to outweigh the worrying thoughts and feelings with happy, positive, relaxing, and calming thoughts and feelings. In the space below, write a list, or make a picture/collage/poster of all of the things that make you feel good, happy, calm, and relaxed. This might also be the things that make you smile and laugh. Think about your different senses too — see, smell, taste, feel, hear. You can use other materials or papers if you want.

You could also turn these things into a happy box, a calming book, or a calming vision board — then you can look at these things when the feelings of worry visit.

Activity 29
Calmness, Peacefulness, Safety, and Relaxation

- Calmness, peacefulness, safety, and relaxation for me, feels like... (choose an image below or choose your own).
- If I gave the feelings of calmness, peacefulness, safety, and relaxation a name/s, it would be...
- If I described the feelings of calmness, peacefulness, safety, and relaxation, it would be...

Activity 30
Exploring and Understanding the Feelings of Safety, Calmness, Relaxation, and Happiness a Bit More

Use Activities 28 and 29 to support you.

Can you think of a specific time and an actual example of when you felt really happy, calm, safe, and relaxed? Can you describe this time in detail (where, when, what, and how)? Maybe you could write it as a story, a poem, a rap, or in a few sentences. If you have a few examples, you can create a whole list or write about all of these different examples. (Use another piece of paper if you need more space.) These are times that you want to bottle up, store in your memory bank, and treasure!

Activity 31
My Very Own Calming Place

One of my favourite calming tricks is when you create a special place that you can travel to in your mind – this is a bit like taking a brain break, or visiting a mind spa. Can you think of a place where you have been, seen, or visited where you felt really happy, calm, safe, peaceful, and relaxed? (You might want to use Activity 24 to help you with some ideas.) This might be your favourite place, a place where you felt super relaxed, calm, and warm inside, a place that makes you smile, and that you would love to go to if you could click your fingers and go to it, or pop into a travel machine and travel back to it.

If so, what was this place called? Or, if you were to choose a name or a title for this place, what would you choose?

_____

When in this place, what can you…

See/notice, look at:
_____
_____

Hear/listen to:
_____
_____

Smell:
_____
_____

Touch/feel/do:
_____
_____

Taste: _____
_____

When you think about or visit in your mind this place...
_____
_____
_____

What do you feel in your body when you are in this place?
_____
_____
_____

What emotions do you feel when you are in this place?
_____
_____
_____

If you had to choose a reminder or a cue word which can help you to remember your special place, what might it be?
_____

If you can't think of a place, that is OK, don't worry – it can be tricky and can take some time. Instead, if you want, you can make up your own magical, fantasy, and imaginary safe place. Try to think of where you would like to travel that could support you to feel happy, relaxed, safe, warm, and so on. Activities 32–35 might help give you some ideas.

You might also like to think about what it might be like if you were going to make this place for an animal or for a favourite friend. Or if you could click your fingers and be anywhere, where would you be? What would you like to see, hear, smell, taste, touch, feel?

Just remember, if you do make up a place, it can be harder to travel back to, so it is important to really describe it, write it down, record it, and make a creative reminder of it (Activities 26–27).

Activity 32
Special and Calming Places

To help you with choosing and thinking about your special place, here are some common places that people have said they use and visit as their safe, calming, happy, relaxing, and soothing place.

Activity 33
Travelling to Your Calming, Safe, and Magical Place

Choosing a way of travelling to your calming place might give you some more time and space to travel there and to make the journey feel a bit more special.

How might you like to travel to your calming, safe, and magical place (circle or colour in the worksheet below)?

Activity 34
Travelling to Your Safe and Special Place

Draw or paint a picture, make a collage, or write a story, song, poem, or rap of how you would like to travel to your special calming place. Use Activity 21 for some inspiration and ideas.

Activity 35
Picture, Song, Rap, Poem, or Story of My Special Place

I hope that now you have found a relaxing and calming place. If you want, you can draw, paint, or make a collage of your special place here (you might want to draw it just as the place, or with you in it). If you prefer, you can use a bigger piece of paper or make a sculpt or a mould of it. You might also like to write a song, rap, poem, or story about visiting your special place.

Activity 36
Reminders and Creative Ways of Showing the Safe Place

Sometimes, when we are feeling full up, fuzzy, stressed, or worried it can be hard to remember or to travel back to our special place. This is one of the reasons why it is helpful to choose a reminder word, to describe our special place in lots of detail, and to practise going to our special place lots of times. To help make your special place even more special, alive, and memorable, you can also make (with an adult's help) a piece of art or a reminder item of your place. It can also be really nice when feeling worried to have a feel-good item to look at and to hold!

There is no right or wrong way to do this, and you might make one, or loads of different ones. Below are some ideas of things which you can do, but the sky is your limit — be as creative as you wish. Other people in your life might have some great ideas too!

Make a pillow of your special place. Use fabric pens on a plain pillowcase, or use photos and get a photo company to make it.

It doesn't need to be a pillow. It could also be on wallpaper or a lamp made up of photos, or on pyjamas, a blanket, etc.

Decorate a teddy bear with photos of your special place, or have a bear where you can put a photo of your place in the face of the bear, or on its t-shirt. You could also use fabric pens to draw your special place on a plain doll or on a doodle doll.

Put your special place on a range of different items, such as a key ring, a snow globe, a pencil case, or your diary.

Use glass pens or go to a photo company to make things like a cereal bowl, a mug, or a plate showing your safe place.

Make a painting, collage, poster, picture, or mosaic of your special place. Then stick or photograph this piece of art, and put it in lots of different places, such as in your diary, next to your bed, or on a keyring.

Make a three-dimensional model, a sculpture, or a mould of your special place using lots of different materials such as clay, miniatures, sand, wood, and shells.

Draw a picture, a painting, or make a mould, or sculpture, of the way you plan to travel to your special place, for example, through a magic fairy gate, or over a bridge (Activity 21).

Activity 37
Special Place Reminder Cards

Now you have a place you can visit to have a little break, here are some cards that you can photocopy, laminate, and carry with you to help you remember your place. It might be helpful for some of the adults who support you to have one too.

⭐ My special place is called ....

⭐ My reminder word is ....

⭐ I travel there by ....

When I am there:

⭐ I can see ....

⭐ I can smell ....

⭐ I can hear ....

⭐ I can feel ....

⭐ I can taste ....

⭐ I feel in my body and mind ....
....

⭐ I will go there when ....

⭐ To help me to go there and to remember I can ....
....

⭐ My special place is called ....

⭐ My reminder word is ....

⭐ I travel there by ....

When I am there:

⭐ I can see ....

⭐ I can smell ....

⭐ I can hear ....

⭐ I can feel ....

⭐ I can taste ....

⭐ I feel in my body and mind ....
....

⭐ I will go there when ....

⭐ To help me to go there and to remember I can ....
....

Activity 38

Sensory, Soothing, Happy, Positive, Calming, and Relaxing Box

Another great Worry Wizard trick is to have your very own calming and happy box/bag/jar. There are step-by-step instructions in the adult section of this book but to get you started, can you think about and fill in the boxes below? You might also like to add some pictures or items to the boxes. For example, if you like to feel silky materials, you might want to find some material and stick it in the feeling box, or if you like to listen to a certain singer, you might want to get their photo and add it to the hearing box!

I like to see	I like to touch/feel
I like to hear	**I like to taste**
I like to smell	**Other things which you like, and which make you feel calm, happy, relaxed, safe, and at peace**

Once you have found some multi-sensory things which make you feel happy, calm, peaceful, and relaxed, you might like to draw or get some pictures, photos, art, cards, quotes, stickers, glitter, and materials to decorate your box. (It doesn't need to be a box if you prefer a different type of container.) Remember, you want to decorate your box in a way that makes you feel happy, calm, and relaxed when you look at it! You might want to give your box its own special name!

Now it's time to fill your box. Take your time. Start small. Look at all of the things which you wrote above that you like to see, hear, smell, taste, and touch; and then think about what you could fill the box with which matches these things. You might already have some things that you know make you feel happier and calmer. The adult reading this with you can help you; you can also make some special things to go inside.

To help you, here are some ideas of what other children have put in their boxes – but remember that everyone is different and these are just some ideas to get you started.

 See – photos, pictures, letters, postcards, strengths cards, coping cards, inspirational quotes, favourite objects, special place reminder or art piece, guardian angel.

 Hear – music, a rain stick, drums, a heartbeat bear, white noise, a bell, wind chime, seashells.

 Smell – perfume, flowers, a candle, aroma dough, cream, smelling oils, balm (remember it needs to be calming).

Touch/do — soft, fluffy, or soothing material, a stress ball, pipe cleaners, feathers, worry dolls, a weighted animal, a dreamcatcher, magic fairy dust, a mandala, a wishing fairy, bubble wrap, play doh, cream, items from nature, a soft toy, a squishy ball, clay, a sensory bottle or bag, a kaleidoscope, a Rubik's cube, a brain teaser game, a puzzle, a fidget toy, a snow globe, colouring-in things, things to sort and organise, such as different coloured buttons/badges/pebbles/stickers/LEGO® pieces.

What would you like to call your box? What items would you like to start with? Remember, the more you use it, and practise using it, the more it will work and be helpful!

Activity 39
Talk Back or Write a Letter to the Worry

Sometimes, it can be great to *talk back* to the worries. You can also use some *positive self-talk*. This is when you say encouraging and supportive words to and about yourself. It can be helpful to think about what the people who like and love you would say to and about you. When you have thought about some, draw the worry in the middle of the page, and then in the speech bubbles write down some feel-good, positive, and encouraging words/statements. For example, 'Go away, worries', 'I don't believe you, worry', 'I'm bigger and stronger than you, worries', 'I'm not going to feed you, worries', 'I can do this', 'I have a whole team of helpers who outweigh you', 'I'm a Worry Wizard with loads of shrinking tricks'. You might also like to *write a letter* to the worry/anxiety telling it to go away, explaining all of your tricks to shrink it, and letting it know all of the people you have on your side helping you!

Activity 40
A Magic Spell

As your very own **Worry Wizard**, you can write a magic spell to vanish and shrink the worries. Think about what your spell or potion would be called: what does it smell like, what words or ingredients would you use in it, and when will you use your magic spell or recipe? (You might like to get some items from the bathroom or kitchen, or from outside to make this magic spell.)

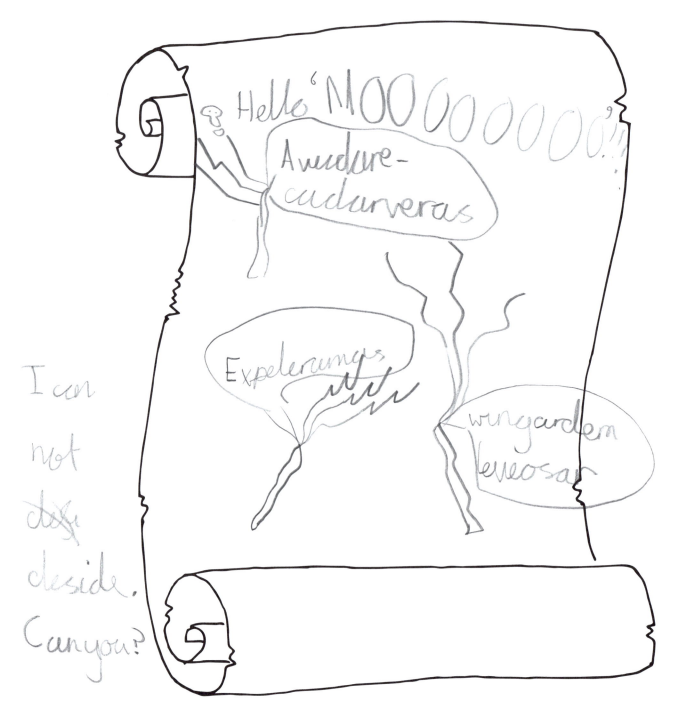

Part 4
Some More Important Messages about Anxiety and Worries

Introduction

At the beginning of Part 2, we learned some important messages about worry and anxiety. Now we are going to learn some more important information about worries and anxiety, including the thoughts, feelings, and behaviours cycle, and then some activities with even more tricks will follow to help you to put this learning into practice. (Adults, see Activities 41–45. Children will need your help understanding the information below. Take your time, and go through it slowly and gradually, in bite-size bits.)

It is important to know that anxiety can at times impact how we think, how we feel in our minds, and in our bodies, and also what we do (our actions and our behaviours). This can lead to a cycle, a domino effect, or a loop, which can feed the anxiety and make us feel worse.

For example, if Tyler, like lots of children do, feels worried about talking in class, he might tell himself and think things like, 'I can't cope', 'Other people will laugh at me', 'I don't have anything important to say'. These negative and critical thoughts (also known as *thinking traps*) might make Tyler feel more worried. Then the more worried he feels, the more this might make his body feel worried, like having a racing heart, feeling panicked, having a stomach ache, and feeling embarrassed and shy. All of these thoughts, feelings, and body sensations then might make Tyler behave in a certain way to try to make the worries smaller and to make himself feel better. For example, he might not talk in class and instead stay quiet, he might leave the class, or if the teacher asks him a question, he might say, 'I don't know', even if he does know.

Here is a diagram to show you how this cycle works:

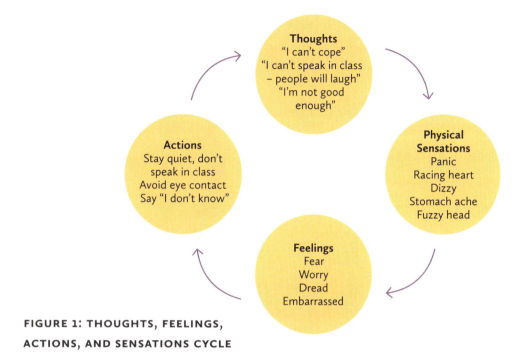

FIGURE 1: THOUGHTS, FEELINGS, ACTIONS, AND SENSATIONS CYCLE

These behaviours and actions can feed the cycle and domino effect even more, as Tyler then feels frustrated at himself for not talking, and he feels worried that the other children still think he has nothing to say. These behaviours also don't give Tyler the chance to practise and to learn to face his fears. So, he doesn't have the opportunity to learn that it is actually OK to talk in the class, and that he does have important things to say, and also, for him to experience that if he does try to practise speaking, it gets easier each time.

This facing the fears is also important as sometimes our thoughts and feelings can feel so strong we listen to them too much! And then we start to believe and think that they are the truth and are facts, but actually, although still super important, they are not facts, they are our thoughts and feelings. For example,

Tyler thought that he couldn't speak up and that he didn't have anything to say, but he later learned through tricks and tools to help him that he could actually do it, and that he did have things to say – even better, he felt super proud of himself that he had managed to face his fear. This made his confidence grow as well.

Sometimes – and this is pretty cool – when we change the way we look at something and how we think about it, it can make a huge difference! For example, if another child looked or stared at Tyler, previously, when the worries were in charge and big, he might have thought that they were looking at him because they thought that he was stupid, or that they were judging him for not talking. But then he changed his thinking to think about the alternatives (other possibilities or other explanations), such as maybe the other child was just looking because they were thinking, or looking into space, or maybe they were looking at him because they liked his pen, or maybe they were looking because they wanted to be his friend, or maybe they were looking at the child behind him, or maybe because they were interested in what he would have to say. Then Tyler could view and think about the other child looking at him in a very different way, in a whole new light, like looking through a different set of glasses or a magic kaleidoscope. This new way of looking in a more positive way changed his thoughts, feelings, sensations, and actions. It changed the loop, the cycle, or the domino effect! Now, that is what I call a cool trick!

So, changing Tyler's thoughts amazingly changed the feelings, thoughts, and behaviours that followed. This is why this workbook is teaching you ways to change this cycle and domino effect, to try things out, and to have tricks to do when you are having thoughts, feelings, or body sensations that make you feel more worried or stop you doing what you want to do.

The next few pages will teach you some ways of looking at the thoughts you have and how this can have a domino effect on your feelings, body, and behaviours. Also, it will give you some ways to try, little by little, to face your fears.

Thinking traps explained

Building on the above, our worries can trick us in a number of ways. They can:

- give us a false alarm, or can make us think, predict, and expect that the worst thing is going to happen, or that we have a magic ball and that we can see into the future. This means we imagine the worst and can blow up the worry/situation to be bigger than it has to be
- trick us to think that we read and see into people's minds and know what they are thinking and feeling about us
- trick us to make the bad and negative things seem much bigger and more powerful than they are. This is like wearing negative glasses which only let you see and focus on the negative things. This also means the worries make the positive and good things harder to see and smaller. So, we pay much more attention to the negative things, like having a negative magnet, and ignore or minimise the good things
- make us think and say negative, horrible, and critical things to and about ourselves
- make us jump to conclusions
- make us think that what we feel or think is the only truth and is a fact
- give us strict and unfair rules like, 'I must…', 'I should…', 'I need to…'
- make us think that something is more likely to happen than it actually is
- make us think in extremes. Sometimes we call this black and white or all-or-nothing thinking. This makes it harder to see all the other colours in between, so sometimes we need to try to think about other alternatives and possibilities.

These are called 'thinking traps'. *Do you think you do any of these?*

One of the things we can do to help and shrink these traps is to try to catch ourselves when we are using or falling into these thinking traps, or for others around us to catch us!

The more we catch them and notice them, the more we can find ways to evaluate these worries and try to find out if we are being tricked. We can try to think and weigh up the advantages and disadvantages. We can think like a judge and assess the facts and evidence for and against the worry/thought/situation. And, we can try to look at the thought/worry/situation from another perspective and angle, like looking through different glasses or a lens/kaleidoscope. The next activities will help you to do that.

Activity 41
Thoughts, Feelings, Body Sensations, and Actions/Behaviours Diary

Can you think of an example of how a worry of yours may fit into the below table? What patterns can you see? What might you learn? Can you see any thinking traps? Use the above information given at the start of Part 4 to support you with this.

Situation/ event (where and when)	Thoughts/ self-talk/ thinking traps	Feelings	Body sensations	Actions/ behaviours

Activity 42
Glasses

It can be helpful to look at a worry/thought/situation/difficulty from lots of different perspectives – different angles. It's like looking at them through a kaleidoscope or through lots of different glasses. Look at the questions below and see if you can apply them to a particular worry or thought. You might want to bring this exercise alive by trying lots of different glasses on while you talk about these. Try to write down your answers, and use the introduction to Part 4 to help you.

Try looking at the worry/though/situation through a different lens

What is the worry saying?

Now what do YOU think/know?

What would a best friend say to you about this worry/situation?

What would you say to a best friend if they had this worry/situation?

Is there another way to look at the worry/situation/thought? (e.g. a more positive, kinder, fairer, or realistic way.)

_____
_____
_____
_____
_____

What thinking traps might you be falling into?

_____
_____
_____

What conclusions and assumptions might you be making?

_____
_____
_____

What is the worst-case scenario?

_____
_____
_____

Is this likely to happen?

_____

Are you expecting and assuming the worst will happen?

_____

If the worst happens, what can you do to cope?

_____
_____
_____

What evidence is there for and against the worry/thought?

_____
_____
_____

Is this thought based on a fact or a feeling?

_____

What is the best-case scenario?

_____
_____
_____

Activity 43
Magic Carpet

Another helpful way, as with the glasses, is to imagine you are flying high on a magic carpet and looking down at the problem/difficulty/worry. If you looked at the worries, fears, and situation from a different place, as if you were travelling high in the sky on a magic carpet ride, looking down, what would you see differently? Sometimes, we need to take a few steps away from the worries and the situation. Draw yourself flying on the magic carpet, and draw or write down the worries or fears which are far beneath you.

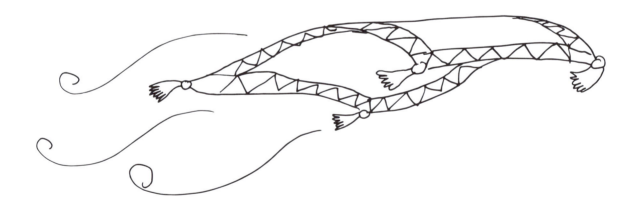

Activity 44
Things You Can Choose and Control, and Things You Can't Control and Choose

Sometimes, we spend a lot of time and energy worrying about things which we cannot control or choose, or things which are not our responsibility. In the circle below, write or draw inside the things which you can control and choose, and on the outside, write down or draw the things you can't control and choose.

Activity 45

Facing Your Fears – Little by Little – The Exposure Ladder

The adult supporting you will help you understand and think through this activity.

As we have learned throughout the story and this workbook, when we feel scared, anxious, or worried, it is normal that we want to do things to get rid of the horrible feeling, or we try to avoid the thing that is making us feel worried and scared. The confusing thing about this is that it usually works quite well, but unfortunately, it is in the short run, and it doesn't last. This is because by avoiding and hiding from the fear, we don't then get the important opportunity of learning that the things which we are scared of are not actually as scary or as powerful as we think they are. By avoiding them, we also don't learn the important lesson that with some time, practice, and help, we can gradually face the fears and make them smaller. This is also important as often the fear of something is scarier than the actual fear! This is especially the case when our mind and body play tricks on us and make us feel that it is scarier than it needs to be.

So, in addition to all of the other tricks and tools in this workbook, another thing that can be really helpful is to write a list of what things worry you.

Once you have this list, break it down into smaller things, and, using a scale, rate them (from 0 being the least scary and 10 being the scariest).

So, for example, someone who is scared of dogs, the least scary for them (we are all different) might be to look at a photograph of a dog, and the scariest might be to touch a dog not on a lead. There will be lots of stages in between, like watching a video of a dog, going to the park where there are dogs, and so on.

Then you are going to be like a scientist and start to experiment. Start at the bottom with the one which you are least afraid of, and slowly and safely, when you are ready and with the help of the adult supporting you and by using some of the tricks you have learned, move up the ladder. Before you do each step, ask yourself, 'What do I think will happen?' Then afterwards, ask yourself, 'What actually happened?' 'What have I learned?' Then celebrate what you have achieved and for trying!

Remember to start really small and move slowly! This way you can build your confidence and feel the success of moving up each step. It is normal to feel worried, but remember, like a wave, the great thing about anxiety is that it will go down! Also, you now have lots of tricks to help you.

The more you do it, the easier it will become, so remember to practise! It can also help to imagine yourself successfully doing the step on the ladder before you do it.

Most Scary

Least Scary

Activity 46
Me as a Worry Wizard

Now you have so many tricks and tools, you might like to draw yourself or decorate a picture of you as a Worry Wizard! What is your Worry Wizard name? What are some of your best powers and tricks?

Me as a Worry Wizard

Activity 47
My Team of Life Helpers

Luckily, Binnie the Baboon has lots of animal friends and helpers, like Raphy the Rhino, Michy the Meerkat, Kace the Kudu, Ellen the Elephant, Gabe the Gorilla, and Chase the Chimp. She felt so much better and not alone when she talked to them about how she felt and got some advice and support from them.

We all need a team of people who can help us — together we are stronger!

Who are your special friends, life cheerleaders, and helpers? Who can you talk to and ask for help and advice? (These can be real, imagined, celebrities, role models, family, friends, neighbours, teachers, professionals, animals, superheroes, and so on. It could be people you know really well or ones you have just met.)

What words of advice and support would they give you?

_____
_____
_____

How do they make you feel?

_____
_____
_____

Make a piece of art — a drawing, sand world, sculpture, mould, or painting — to show all of your life cheerleaders, inspirers, and supporters — your special team! They are the people who can help you to outnumber and outsmart the worries. The examples below use puppets, miniatures, ink, and a people photo blanket!

Activity 48
Overcoming Challenges

It can be great, especially when the worries have tricked you to think you can't do it, to remember that you are strong, brave, real, and special — and that you have overcome some changes, new things, obstacles, or challenges, whether small or big.

Soon — maybe even already! — the worries can be added to this important list.

First, with the help of the adults who support you, and who know you best, write down in the box a list of these things. Then you can draw, sculpt, mould, or write down all of the different things you have overcome, navigated, conquered, and made it through. You can make this even more creative and fun by showing these things which you have overcome and navigated through by using things like mountains, an obstacle course, a maze, and so on. Some examples are shown below.

A list of some of the changes, transitions, challenges, and obstacles I have overcome...

Activity 49
Me Shrinking and Becoming Freer from the Worries and Anxiety – I Can Do It!

Draw, write about, make, or sculpt you against the worries — facing them, shrinking them, and vanishing them. This could be lots of different ways, there is no right or wrong way; but it might be you getting unstuck from the worry web, or you free from the worry weights, or you climbing over or around the worry wall, or using your tricks on the worries.

Give it a title or a catchphrase too! You might want to do more than one piece of art.

Activity 50
Sentence Completion

Complete the following sentences (you can draw or act out your answers if you prefer):

I shrunk my worries by...

I made my worries go away by...

I am bigger and stronger than the worries because...

I have learned about myself that...

I am proud of myself because...

When I feel worried now, I can make my worries smaller by...

Now that I have some Worry Wizard tricks, I feel...

My favourite Worry Wizard trick is...

I am still going to work on...

Sometimes, it can help us remember if we write down and record all of our favourite coping strategies, tricks, and positive messages. One way you can do this is to draw around your hand and write down a trick or message to remember on each finger and on your thumb. Then you can keep this drawing with you or look at your actual hand as a reminder. I call this a Protective Palm. Another way is to write them down on a treasure box or on a wizard's hat (these activities follow if you would like to do that).

Activity 51
Treasure Box of Tools, Tricks, and Coping Gems

On this treasure box, you can write down or draw all of your different tricks, tools, and coping gems.

Activity 52

My Favourite and Most Helpful Worry Wizard Tricks and Tools

Write down and/or draw all of your different and favourite Worry Wizard magic tricks and coping tools.

My Worry Wizard Tricks and Tools

Activity 53
Escape the Worry Maze

Find your way through the maze, just like you have escaped and worked your way through the worries.

Activity 54
Certificate of Worry Wizardry

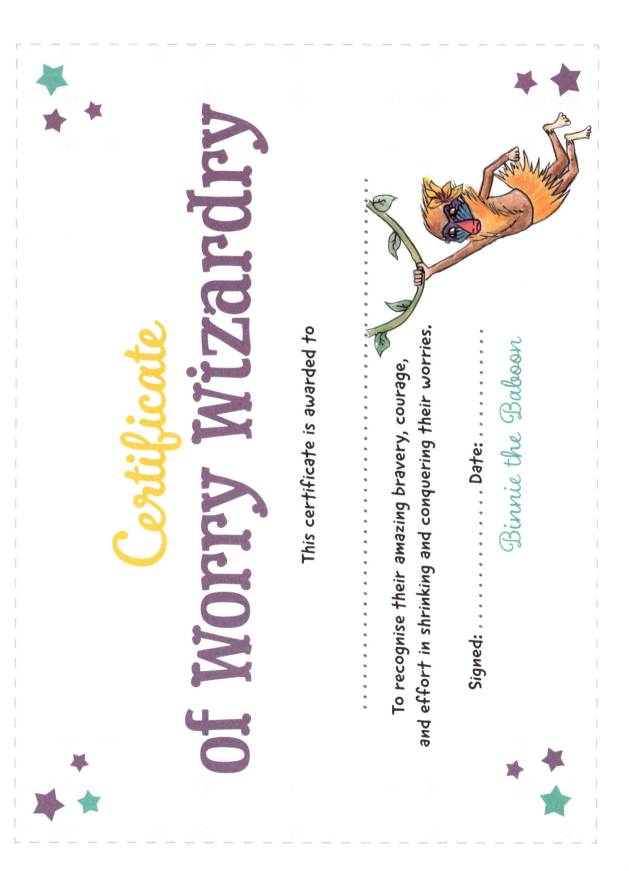

Guide for Adults

Introduction to the workbook and important information about how to use it

This book is intended to give you lots of ideas and strategies in order to strengthen children's (and your own) ability to regulate, calm down, relax, and develop effective and useful coping strategies, particularly in the context of worry, fear, nervousness, anxiety, and stress.

Some children will simply enjoy the story of Binnie the Baboon as a stand-alone story, and it will be helpful and fun in itself. Some may benefit from trying one or two of the included activities, while others – particularly those who are experiencing frequent feelings of worry, anxiety, fear, nervousness, and stress – will most likely benefit from doing the majority of the activities, in addition to other supplementary tasks and interventions. For this reason, some pages in this book have been designed to be photocopiable, so that if you wish, you can select the suitable activities and give them to the child separately or stapled together to make their own personalised book. This also means that the same activity can be used several times to target different situations or stages.

With this in mind, before you start the activity book, it can be helpful to read the story a few times, and then to ask the child some questions about Binnie in order to prepare the context and to gain an understanding of their grasp of the story and the more general topics covered around relaxation, anxiety, stress, worry, coping skills, and so on.

This sets the scene and gives you an initial understanding as to where the child is at, and also helps you to give them reasons as to why you are going through the activity book with them, and why it might be helpful. The more they understand the rationale and have a sense of the potential benefits of the workbook, the more engaged they will be. This is also where the adults supporting them to go through the workbook need to express verbally and non-verbally their hope, belief, and enthusiasm about the benefits and process of the book.

In addition, to accommodate the huge range of children and adults who will be reading this book, I have intentionally offered different exercises for each activity. For example, when talking about feeling stuck and overwhelmed, I have given options of a worry web, a worry wall, and worry weights (and these are just suggestions – there could be ones which you and the child choose that fit much better for them as an individual). This variety, again, is to offer diversity and choice, and to acknowledge the uniqueness of each child. Together, you and the child you are supporting can choose which exercises are the most appealing and relevant to them.

It is overwhelming to do all of the activities, and generally not necessary, so try to take your time, be selective, and tailor them – this is why it is helpful for you to familiarise yourself with the options first.

Each child is unique

The ideas in this workbook are intended to offer guidance and suggestions; they are not prescriptive or exhaustive in any way. Each child will inevitably respond to the story and the activities that follow differently, just as each one of us responds differently to experiences. We are all unique. Factors affecting their responses might include their age and developmental stage, their interests, their life experiences, their relationships with the adult reading with them, the cause of their worries/fears, and their overall cognitive ability. So, please feel free to take the ideas in this book and to use your own creativity to apply them sensitively to meet your child's needs.

For example, you'll see that I will often prompt to encourage communication in a form that isn't just writing or drawing – children can sculpt, experiment, act, build structures, use animation packages, and so on. The more creative and alive it feels to them, the more successful the activities will be! Kids learn best when having fun, and that applies to when doing the activities in this book! For example, it is much easier to talk about worry when building a worry tower, or talking of metaphors like a worry web, than it is sitting down and making it feel like schoolwork.

What sort of environment works best?

The activities should ideally be tried when the child is in a 'thinking and learning space' – not when they are tired, hungry, distracted, or distressed. They also should be done at a time when the child and adult are not going to be rushed, and have the time and energy needed to be fully present. The child, even more in the context of anxiety, needs to know and feel verbally and non-verbally that there is no right or wrong, good or bad, and that they are safe to share whatever feelings they have, and that their feelings are valid, heard, seen, and important.

Guide for Adults

Who should use this book, what are some of the benefits, and why?

This activity book is intended to be used by someone who has a positive and safe relationship with the child, such as a parent, caregiver, therapist, educational professional, social worker, or residential worker. This book is likely to be particularly useful for and is tailored to those children who experience anxiety, worries, stress, fear, and nervousness. However, this book is likely to have something for everyone, as we all want our children to be as happy, confident, and worry-free as possible.

Worrying is something that we all experience, and all children benefit from further understanding their feelings, thoughts, and worries, and then actively learning some internal and external coping strategies, and from having a range of buffers to protect them against the impact of stressors and worries.

Navigating life and daily situations can be messy, difficult, and complex. So, enabling children to have some skills, options, and 'go-to' tools helps to give them the best opportunity to cope with these, and to know how to respond and navigate them. It is like giving them an internal compass, especially as children will often be in situations, such as at school or with their peers, when they do not have their parent or carer physically with them. So, the more they have absorbed, internalised, integrated, and practised these skills on a regular basis in their day-to-day life, within a positive relationship, the more they will feel equipped, resourced, and prepared to use them.

Not a substitute for therapy

It is important to mention, that while this workbook is written by a clinical psychologist and is therapeutic in nature, it is not a substitute for therapy or for a formal clinical intervention. Should the need for a formal intervention be indicated, you are advised to seek professional advice. As you read certain activities, you will have a sense of whether they are suitable for the child you are supporting, or whether they feel too complex. Only do what you and the child feel comfortable doing.

Structure of the book

Following on from the Binnie the Baboon illustrated story, there are a series of activities for the child to complete, and to be able to dip into. These range from word searches, to quizzes, to colouring-in exercises, through to activities intended to support children to recognise, label, and understand their worries and fears. Then there are a series of worksheets and activities to help them (with adult support) with reducing their worries, stress, and fears, and finding and learning a range of coping strategies and resources. Some of these can be completed by the child alone, particularly the fun activities; however, their magic and effectiveness are likely to be much greater if done with a grown-up, and in a positive and trusting relationship. After all, feeling supported, important, listened to, seen, heard, held, and understood by another person is the most powerful experience and ingredient.

This adult section of the book gives you lots of additional tips, ideas, and activities for supporting this process, and for understanding how worries work, which is why it is important to read it *first*. The more comfortable the adult reading the workbook is, the more comfortable the child will feel.

Order of activities and tasks

It is important to remember that while this book has been written with an order and sequence in mind, it is not intended to be offered as a step-by-step programme or manual. Some children might skip a bunch of exercises, only do one or two activities, or only find one section helpful, dip in and then dip out, whereas others might find it fun and useful to go through each activity. This is why it is important for the supporting adult to read through this book first and to familiarise themselves with it, as well as to know the individual child.

Now that this workbook has been introduced, some key messages to hold in mind about worries and anxiety will be introduced.

Tips about reading this section

- Pick your moment to read this section, ideally one when you are in a good thinking space, and not being distracted. Circle or underline key points.
- Take your time, as some of them are big and may be unfamiliar concepts. The more you understand them and think about them, the more equipped and confident you will feel to explain them to the child.
- Be kind, forgiving, and compassionate to yourself. Parenting or supporting a child, particularly one in distress, is a mammoth task.
- Try to reflect on the questions asked. The more we have a sense and an understanding, the more we can help a child have more understanding and clarity. The questions will give you lots of ideas and tips for how to support the child with the activities. We can also anticipate and plan for potential obstacles and questions we may face.
- Revisit the sections (after all, repetition is key for remembering, learning, and processing, and each time you will notice, read, and think about something different).
- You might like to make a poster, a crib sheet, a refrigerator note, a collage, a chart of the key points and put them in your own words. This can support you in processing the material, and to see it in a more visual way, and make it fit for you.
- You also might like to keep a diary or record of which ones you are going to try to do/are already doing/want to think about.
- Please note these are not presented in order of importance.

What is anxiety and worry, and what are the key messages about anxiety and worry?

WHY IS HAVING AN UNDERSTANDING IMPORTANT AND HELPFUL?

The terms worry and anxiety are clinically and academically different; however, for the purposes of this workbook, rather than get into a definitional maze, some information on both, including related words, such as stress and nervousness, will be briefly described. The focus of this section is not to give a detailed account and a diagnostic list, but rather to offer the reader an increased understanding of some of the feelings, thoughts, sensations, and patterns associated with anxiety and worry, as well as some key messages to hold in mind about them. This understanding is key before going through the workbook, as it will support the reader in having more information to explain in child-friendly terms to the child, but also will, I hope, increase the reader's empathy, perspective-taking, and knowledge, which in turn can impact their reactions and responses, with the aim of making them as supportive and helpful as possible. Additionally, the more we understand something, the less overwhelming, confusing, and unmanageable it can feel, and the more we can start to match our response to the why.

This is also important because anxiety and worry can feel scary and overwhelming, so it can feel as if it picks up power like a tornado! Other metaphors to explain this are likened to a worry web which spins and knots even more, or a backpack which gets heavier and heavier each time more worry weights are added, making things feel harder, more tiring, and more effortful. Therefore, the more we support children to understand what is happening, to express it, and to have strategies to reduce it, the more they can be supported to have a way out of the worry web, to empty out some of the worry backpack, or to slow the tornado down. This makes the worries feel less overwhelming and supports them to feel more in control, more confident, and better equipped.

HOW DO WORRIES SHOW THEMSELVES, AND SOME OF THE DIFFERENCES WITHIN THIS?

At any age and across the life span, feeling worried, and at times anxious, stressed, or nervous, is completely normal, common, and expected. Worries can come in many different forms. They can be specific, such as worrying about a particular incident, or they can be more general, for example a general feeling of worry and of being on edge. They can also be more focused around a particular area, such as worrying about one's health (e.g. health anxiety) or worries about leaving a caregiver (e.g. separation anxiety), or worrying about social occasions and interactions (e.g. social anxiety).

Worries can seem unrelated and confusing and hard to place or understand, or, more typically, they can be based on something children/adults feel, have seen, have heard, have been told, have imagined, or have experienced. Certain worries are also more expected and typical depending on the child's age and stage. For example (of course this varies according to the individual and the context), a toddler is more likely to worry about being separated from their caregiver, about scary monsters, and about the dark; a teenager is more likely to worry about fitting in, their appearance, and school pressures.

Moreover, worrying thoughts and feelings can be fleeting, temporary, and short lived, or for those children struggling more, they can be much more pervasive, chronic, and long term. Their frequency, severity, and impact on the child and on their lives and the people around them tends to be on a spectrum. The impact the anxiety has is often the most important part in terms of thinking about what type or level of support is needed, for example if the worries are feeling overwhelming to the child, are causing them frequent distress, and are stopping them from doing things.

Additionally, worry/anxiety can show itself in lots of different physical, sensory, cognitive, and emotional ways, and every individual and the context they live in is unique. Some children will be able to express how they feel; others won't have the words, or will struggle for a variety of reasons to find the words. Similarly, for some children, the worry may come out as a worry, but for others, it can show itself in other forms, such as sadness, shyness, or irritability. It is important to know the individual child and recognise their different ways of expression, because anxiety and worries often underlie a lot of other forms of distress and behaviours we might see. For example, anger is generally seen as being an emotion that is married to fear or sadness. It is helpfully viewed as a bodyguard and mask emotion.

This said, there are some more common ways anxiety and worry can be expressed and can impact a child. The symptoms are often in line with what one would expect with the tasks of child development. So, we need to consider how frequent, severe, and impactful the symptoms are, particularly compared with what one might expect for the age and stage of the child. Some children may experience just one, others might experience several. This is not an exhaustive list:

Body-based, physical and sensory symptoms:

- Trembling/shaking.
- Tense/stiff.
- Heart beating faster/racing heart.
- Floppy/flimsy/like jelly.
- Weak/dizzy/light-headed/tingling/spinning head.
- Headaches/heavy head.
- Fuzzy head/difficult to think, concentrate, or pay attention.
- A feeling of dread.
- Panic.
- Tight chest/struggling to breathe/breathing fast/short of breath.
- Stomach ache/butterflies in tummy/running tummy/knots in tummy.
- Needing to go to the toilet or being constipated.
- Change in appetite, for example hungry/not hungry.
- Change in sleep, struggling to sleep, sleeping too much.
- Sweating/feeling hot/feeling red.
- Feeling cold/frozen.
- Dry mouth, feeling thirsty.
- Blurred vision.
- Talking very quickly/racing mind/whirling thoughts/struggling to speak.
- Feeling on edge/restless/fidgety/pacing.
- Stuttering and stammering.
- Grinding teeth.
- Rashes or skin problems.

Cognitive, emotional, and behavioural symptoms:

- Ruminating, looping, and racing thoughts (e.g. a tornado or tumble dryer of thoughts and worries whirling around. This can also be likened to feeling stuck in a loop of thoughts, like a broken record player, or a hamster in a wheel).
- Negative and critical thoughts. These might include underestimating one's ability to cope, expecting oneself to be unsuccessful, overestimating the likelihood of bad, scary, or dangerous things happening, anticipating the worst-case scenario. The section below on thinking traps will expand on this further.
- Reducing, stopping, or avoiding behaviours and situations which might trigger fear. So, the worries can stop children from doing and achieving things. This might include withdrawing or hiding from people/situations/places/the trigger.
- Struggling to focus and struggling to concentrate and attend, often to anything but the thing that is worrying them. So, the worry becomes the thing that feels big and dominates.
- Being fidgety/pacing/restless/feeling tense/achy/struggling to sit still.
- Excessive worries and fears including what-ifs and I can'ts.
- A feeling of dread, doubt, impending doom, or of being in danger.
- Feeling out of control/powerless/helpless, and needing to try to find ways to regain control.
- Walking away or leaving situations/planning escape routes and ways out.
- Asking for reassurance and seeking approval (more than one would expect for a child of that age).
- Feeling under pressure/overly high expectations of self/perfectionism.
- Feeling unsure, uneasy, apprehensive, lacking in confidence.
- Checking for danger/mistakes/threat.
- Sensitive/vigilant/hyper-aware of other people's responses, to one's own actions, and to situations.
- Expressing feelings of worry or fear.
- Worry can also come out as sadness/tearfulness/neediness/anger/sensitivity/irritability.
- Nightmares or sleep difficulties (see my *Neon the Ninja Activity Book* for more on this).
- Finding change, transitions, and new things tricky.
- Engaging in rituals and rules.
- Bottling things up.
- Expressing specific phobias, for example dogs.
- Experiencing signs of panic, which may take the form of a panic attack.

The above signs and symptoms can understandably show themselves differently depending on the type of anxiety. For example, if a child is experiencing health anxiety, then these will show themselves more around areas related to health and they may experience things such as worrying about getting sick or dying, being hypervigilant and sensitive to their body, predicting that the worst will happen to them, being preoccupied by thoughts about illness and health, worrying that something healthwise will be missed, and so forth.

WHY CAN WORRIES FEEL SCARIER TO CHILDREN?
As said previously, feeling worried is completely normal, common, and expected. We all feel these emotions at different times, and these are OK and need to be acknowledged and validated. We also need to support children to name and express them. However, worries can feel bigger for a child. There are lots of reasons for this, but one of them is because most experiences are new and novel for a child, so they inevitably are filled with lots of uncertainty and unknowns. Children generally have more active imaginations than adults, and are often more influenced by what they see, learn, hear, and feel around them!

Children also often struggle more with recognising their feelings and sensations, because these might be new and they haven't had practice or opportunities to develop a cognitive framework around them or to develop an emotional dictionary for describing them. So, they may think that there is something really 'wrong' with them or make assumptions that the worry will last forever. They also might feel weird, weak, out of control, or worry about going crazy, which can add to the worry and the sense of self-consciousness. This is another reason why worries can feel scarier but also why awareness, recognition, and understanding are so important.

Also, children have not yet developed the same memory bank that adults have. When they feel unsure or in need, they can't revisit a memory bank and a history gallery of events that shows and reminds them of all of the times that they have felt worried or tried something new, and it turned out OK, and they found they could do it. They also often haven't yet developed or mastered a repertoire of coping tools, buffers, and strategies which they can refer to and try out in times of need. This is another reason why they need the adults around them to model and teach these, and practise these with them.

Moreover, children often haven't yet developed a robust cognitive framework that can support them in the moment and afterwards to problem solve, rationalise, and make sense of what is happening to them; and then be able to talk and navigate themselves through the worry. This is also why adult support is so important. Within this, children also tend to function more in their emotional brains, and also live much more in the present moment (now rather than future thinking); so, for them, putting things into perspective, and using their thinking, logical, and rational brains can be harder.

Additionally, children often don't have the rich emotional vocabulary needed to describe and make sense of their feelings and of their sensations, which can then make their feelings and body sensations feel scarier, more confusing, and more overwhelming. This is one of the reasons why helping children to develop a language to describe and name their feelings, and to make the mind-body links (e.g. butterflies in my tummy might mean I am worried and/or excited) can be so helpful and important. Then, once they have a language to describe it, they can be supported to learn some skills to reduce the worries. The sections which follow on emotional regulation and naming feelings, and several of the activities within the workbook, provide support with this.

Understanding a bit more about the processes and thinking patterns which can perpetuate and reinforce the anxiety – a cognitive behavioural therapy cycle

This section is key for supporting the child in Activities 41–45.

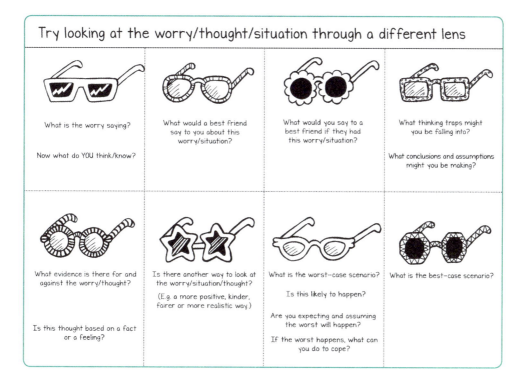

For some children, when they experience worries and anxiety, particularly those which are more chronic and pervasive, they can unfortunately develop more negative, doubting, and more critical self-beliefs and thoughts (e.g. 'I'm stupid', 'I can't do it', 'Bad things are going to happen', 'I'm not good enough'). These beliefs and thoughts inevitably shape and guide the way they see themselves and are often the lens and mirror through which they are likely to frame and judge situations, interactions, and experiences. Like a kaleidoscope, it colours how they see things and it gives them a unique perspective on how to make sense of things, notice, and respond to them (see Activity 42). For example, think about how differently a child who thinks, 'Bad things are going to happen to me, and I can't cope', when something small happens, and how they might feel/react to a minor event, compared with a child who is not expecting or assuming bad things will happen, and who feels more confident and able to cope.

These negative thoughts and beliefs can feel stronger than others and so we might use our negative glasses to pay more attention to them, to give them more weight, and to look for evidence to confirm them. This is a bit like having a negative powered-up magnet. If you think about it, most of us pay more attention to negative information. If ten people tell you that you look lovely, but one person says you look horrible, which one tends to stick? This is because for most of us, good things can be easily lost like falling through a sieve, and bad stuff can stick like glue. This is even more the case if we already are more sensitive and aware of the negative thought – then we pay more attention to it. For instance, think about when you buy or are thinking of buying a new car, and suddenly you notice lots more of those cars on the road; or when you are pregnant or trying to get pregnant, suddenly you see and notice bumps and prams and babies everywhere. The more we pay attention, the more we notice and see things. This is called having an attentional bias. It is the same for negative and worrying thoughts – the more we pay attention to them, the more we notice and feed them, and then we also often look and add evidence to confirm them (known as a confirmation bias).

These thoughts and beliefs also can lead to a negative and perpetuating cycle or a domino effect. For example, we might feel panicked and so worry that we are going to faint, and then because we are paying more attention to our body, and expecting to faint, and telling ourselves that we are going to faint, this inevitably makes us panic even more, which makes us feel more faint, which feeds the thought and makes it stronger, 'I'm going to faint'.

Also, because of these thoughts, the child/adult often starts to develop rules and assumptions to live by according to this belief (they are often unaware of these rules and assumptions). For instance, a rule might be, 'Because I'm stupid, I must never make mistakes' and an assumption might be, 'I'll never be good enough, whatever I do'. This inevitably has a ripple effect and can lead to an unhelpful cycle, involving, for example, not trying new things, spending too much time checking things so that they don't make a mistake that they miss doing other things, or getting so upset and feeling hopeless if they do make a mistake. This negative cycle is explained in cognitive behavioural therapy (a type of short-term therapy based on the cognitive and behaviour model) and is shown visually in Figure 2.

So, for example, something happens (an event/situation), and then the child tells themselves something, which can make them feel something, which in turn leads them to take an action or to do something. This is also key, as what often happens with anxiety and in worrying situations is that it is a human reaction to try to avoid/stop/reduce the thing that is making you feel worried. This is sometimes the best option, and it works, especially in the short term. The concerning part is that it generally doesn't work in the long term, because the child doesn't have the opportunity to face their fears and to learn that it can be better. So, often, the fear becomes bigger or certainly is not reduced – there is fear of the fear (Activity 45). For example, if a child is worried about speaking in class, by not speaking in class, the fear is often reduced, but then they also miss out on opportunities. They don't learn that it will probably be OK to speak in class, and if they don't do it for so long, the thought of it feels and becomes even scarier. Also, the more they don't speak, the more other children might comment or notice that they are not speaking, which feeds the fear even more.

Building on the above, what often happens in these situations is that we look for information to reinforce and confirm our feelings/fears/thoughts; and become more alert and sensitive to cues. So, for example, we might interpret someone looking at us in the class as them thinking we are stupid, rather than considering another possible explanation, such as they like our hairband or they are simply looking around the classroom. Or, we might feel a little tummy flutter because we are scanning and being super attentive to our body, but it might worry us more and then we start to feel the flutters frantically flying around in there, which in turn can make the situation feel much scarier than it needs to be.

So, in essence we want children to experience in a gradual stepped way (often referred to in cognitive behavioural therapy as exposure) that they can do these things. This small-step approach respects and validates the child's feelings and fears. It does not push the child too far or into an anxiety-provoking situation until they are ready; instead, it builds on the success of the last step and helps them to grow in confidence with each step (see Activity 45 for instructions on how to do this).

This is also important as often the prediction and anticipation of something is worse than the actual event itself, and when children slowly try things out, they learn that with some help, they can do it, and if they feel worried or anxious, it is OK and expected and the feelings of anxiety, like a wave, will go down eventually. They learn to ride the waves.

Therefore, the idea is that if we can change one part of the cycle, such as our thoughts/feelings/sensations/reactions to it, it will have a ripple effect on the other parts and reduce the impact (see Activities 41–45).

FIGURE 2: THOUGHTS, FEELINGS, ACTIONS, AND SENSATIONS CYCLE

Take a moment to read the above slowly and in small sections. Try to refer to your own thoughts and feelings. Look at Activities 41–45. The more you understand these concepts and ideas, the more you will be able to empathise and understand the child's experience and find ways to explain it to them.

In addition, in cognitive behavioural therapy, these negative rules, assumptions, and beliefs are often referred to as 'thinking traps' (we all do them at times). Some of these thinking traps are described in the box below. Many of them overlap and interweave with each other. As you are reading them, think about which ones might apply to you and the child you are supporting. The more we 'catch' ourselves using them or support children to 'catch' themselves falling into one of these traps, the more we can understand them, reduce them, try to find solutions, and make fairer assumptions (see Activity 42 for a discussion on this).

Some common thinking traps of worry and anxiety

Mental filtering: magnifying the negative and minimising the positive – This is where we pay more attention to certain evidence, usually the negative, and subsequently minimise, ignore, disqualify, or discount the positive. For example, 'My presentation was rubbish' (even though there was an overwhelming positive response); 'Did you see Jacob rolling his eyes and laughing?' (magnifying the one negative). Or, if a child thinks, 'I'm a failure', they might pay attention to all the times that they don't do well in their football game, but discount or minimise the times that they actually do well. They might also put their success down to luck, a fluke, or someone else's actions. They might say, 'It was an easy game', 'The others didn't try', 'It was all because of Adam', or 'It was pure luck'.

All-or-nothing or black and white thinking – For example, 'I'm such a scaredy cat, so there's no point in even trying'; 'I'm too different – I'll never have any friends'.

Mind-reading – This is where we make an assumption that we know what someone else is thinking or feeling, for example, 'I know no one will like me', 'She thinks I'm stupid'.

Negative self-labelling and negative self-talk – Labelling or talking about oneself negatively or critically. For example, 'I'm a loser', 'I'm pathetic'.

Overgeneralising – This is where a child interprets one event as a generalised pattern. For example, 'I didn't do well in that test; it's because I'm rubbish at schoolwork', or after one wobble in the playground, saying, 'I don't want to go to school; I can't cope in the playground.'

Catastrophising and focusing on the worst-case scenario – 'I forgot a word in my speech. Everyone thinks I am stupid – I'll never have any friends', 'I will fall on my face and lose the race', 'That person touched me; I am going to get sick'.

Negative comparisons with others – For example, 'She's so much better than me'; 'Nathan doesn't struggle making friends and playing football; he's so much cooler and more confident than me'.

Fortune-telling/future-reading – 'If I join the race, I'll lose, so there's no point even taking part', 'I know I won't get picked for the school play', 'I know I'll embarrass myself tonight'.

As stated above, these thinking traps can be very helpful to explain to children in child-friendly ways and then to support them to catch themselves when using one of them on a regular basis. In addition, they can be used to support children to think of a kinder and fairer alternative, verdict, or conclusion, and to investigate, problem solve, and evaluate the accuracy of the belief or assumption. Activities 41–46 can help you in doing this.

What are common things that children worry about and fear?

As said previously, every child is unique, and many of the things they worry about might interweave and overlap. The image here shows some (it is not an exhaustive list) of the common worries and fears. Some of these are much more typical and expected of certain age groups, such as a toddler with separation anxiety, or a teenager who wants to fit in and worries about their appearance. These are also broad categories and the important bit is knowing the richness of the detail. So, it is important that if you identify one of these worries, you try to find out more about what this looks like and means to the specific child. Some questions will follow to support you to do this, and Activities 7–19 will also aid these discussions.

Questions to expand on understanding the worries/anxiety

The above categories are helpful to get a general sense of the type of worry. However, as said previously, it is the richness and the detail which will help you understand the worry a bit more, and the more you understand it, the less overwhelming it can feel to both you and the child, and the more you can try to find ways together to problem solve and reduce it. Activities 7–19 will support you to understand and help the child expand on their worries. However, the following questions are also useful to keep in mind (some will help you, but wouldn't be appropriate to directly ask), to ask, to observe, to think about, to reflect on, or to gently, sensitively, and gradually explore.

- *What is the actual worry/anxiety? What does it look like/feel like? Can you give a specific example with details of when the worry/anxiety happened?*
- *Can you describe a typical day, and how the worry shows itself?*
- *How does this worry/anxiety look in relation to other children of their age?*
- *When did the worry/anxiety start, and how frequently does the worry occur? Why might the worry/anxiety have started at that time?*
- *What is the child's relationship with and history to worry/anxiety? Where might they have seen it, learned it from, developed it, felt it, needed it?*
- *Where does the worry/anxiety occur? Are there differences depending on the context/place/people present?*
- *What other variables and factors impact the worry/anxiety? Are there particular patterns to the worry/anxiety? It can be helpful to track, map out, chart, and/or or note in a diary the patterns of the worry/anxiety. Consider what happened before, during, and after the behaviour. (See Activities 15 and 41.)*
- *What triggers, hotspots, variables (e.g. environmental, sensory, autobiographical, physical, cognitive, relational, emotional, situational) make the worries bigger, smaller, absent, present, and so on? Are there ways in which the triggers could be reduced?*
- *What happens in the times when the worry is absent or less? What is different and why? How can these times be increased, magnified, and celebrated?*
- *What impact does this worry/anxiety have on them, others, and their life?*
- *What is the worry/anxiety making trickier or stopping the child/adults from doing? (See Activity 21.)*
- *What do we think the worry/anxiety might be communicating? What functions is it serving? What might the story be behind the behaviour and underneath the surface?*

- *If the worry/anxiety could talk/had a voice, what might it say?*
- *What might it look like/feel like (advantages and disadvantages) if the worry disappeared or was absent?*
- *What strategies/interventions have been tried already? What bits of these were helpful or less helpful and why?*
- *What responses/reactions from others has the child had when showing the worry/anxiety?*
- *What skills do we think are needed to reduce the worry/anxiety? Does the child need these skills taught, modelled, and practised?*

SCALING QUESTIONS

Sometimes when finding out more about the feelings it is also helpful to support children to identify how much they feel the feeling. This helps them to share and notice the intensity of the feeling and differentiate different types of feelings. Common questions include using a rating scale, so, for example, 'If 0 was cool as a cucumber, and 10 was super super worried, where would you place yourself?' If a child says, for example, 3, it is useful to find out what 3 looks like, feels like, and means to them. Also, it is useful to explore what is keeping them at a 3 instead of a 0, 1, or 2. This helps to identify some of the things that are going well – the protective factors. Then you can explore what they think might help them to move to a 5 or 6. Scaling can be made more child-friendly and fun by using props and regulating activities, such as play doh, LEGO® blocks (as seen in the photos), or different shades of food colouring. Also, things like thermometers or ladders can be used.

We have briefly discussed some of the common worries, some of the key messages around anxiety and worries, some of the symptoms and presentations of worry, a few of the reasons why the worries continue, and some questions for understanding worries more. Now we can look at a few key parenting/intervention positions and tips for optimising our response to children.

Top tips for responding to worry and anxiety

Of course, these are not exhaustive or prescriptive and will vary depending on the individual child, adult, relationship, and the frequency/impact/nature/severity of the worry itself.

These brief tips will be expanded on further in the following sections.

- Try to stay as calm and as grounded as possible. We need to aim to be the rainbow in the child's storm. We need to try to add to the calm rather than getting sucked into the emotional quicksand or the emotional tornado. Of course, this is easier said than done!
- Truly try to listen and hear the worry. Try not to tell the child that they are being silly or they should stop being anxious. They need their feelings validated and noticed, and not to feel judged and alone. One of the ways to help you with this is to try to shrink yourself to the child's size to see the world from their perspective, and to try to remember how you would feel or have felt when someone told you that your feelings were silly, or you should just stop feeling them.
- Lead by example. Try to model to the child and teach them different ways of expressing themselves, and that it is OK to have a range of feelings – we are human! Remember that children learn and absorb from watching and feeling how others express themselves and respond. As Gandhi says, 'Be the change you want to see'.
- Try to be as measured in your response as possible – we don't want to over-react or to make the worry/situation feel too big or too unmanageable. This is particularly important as emotions are contagious and children pick up on how we are feeling. We want children to feel as contained as possible and to feel that they are in safe hands.
- Where possible, normalise that worries are OK, are normal, are common, and are expected. Tell them and show them that they are not alone, and that everyone has worries. In the story, Binnie found it reassuring and comforting to know that she wasn't alone or strange, and that all of the other animals were dealing with or had also grappled with worries and stressors. They need to know that sometimes these worries can be helpful and can be our friends (Activity 20).
- Separate the children from the problem/worry/difficulty. Use person/child-first language. They are not a worrier, but someone who has some worries. To create this distance, it can be helpful to add a 'the' instead of 'you' or 'your' ('the worries'), and to give the worries a name. The more separate the problem feels, the more the child will look at it with some perspective and see that together you will be able to conquer it. Activities 8 and 22 support you to begin to do this.
- Pay attention, notice, magnify, and celebrate the child's strengths, skills, and resiliencies. They are so much more than the worry! We want their wall of strengths and skills to overpower their worry wall!
- Hold the hope. Show them that you are there to problem solve together and to help them through it, and are confident that things can and will get better.

Modelling and leading by example

Supporting adults should aim to lead by example, and teach, normalise, show, and model to children different ways of making sense of feelings and of responding to them (the whole range of feelings). This is key as children are sponges and take in so much of what they see, feel, and observe.

This also includes adults actively modelling how to make sense of and respond to these feelings and situations, ideally in a calm, thoughtful, and regulated way (this, of course, is easier said than done). This includes being mindful of our body language, tone of voice, and our facial expressions, as these non-verbal cues are as important, if not more important than our words. This doesn't mean not reacting, as children benefit from learning that emotions are safe to show and share; but rather being more intentional about how these are expressed; and aware that children are absorbing what they feel and see from us.

This is also important as children are so attuned to these different ways of communication and it is through these interactions that children start to learn and develop tools and ways of expressing, communicating, and responding to different emotions and arousal states. This fits with the commonly used parenting saying, 'The way we treat them teaches them'. Therefore, we need to model the model. Ask yourself:

- *How am I teaching children that all emotions are OK and acceptable and valid, and that they can be heard and felt and shared, without them feeling overwhelmed by them?*
- *What are they learning about how I react which they can take forward to how they could react?*
- *What skill and message do I want children to learn and take forward from this experience/situation?*
- *What skill and message am I trying to teach and show them in this moment?*
- *What feelings, sensations, words, facial expressions, actions are they likely to be hearing, feeling, and seeing from me and other people around them about anxiety, worries, and calmness?*
- *If they were asked how different people in their life react to stressful situations, what do you think they say?*
- *How would I like them to respond to...if they were at school, or not with me?*

Therefore, as hard, exhausting and stressful as it is, and accepting that we are all human and will make 'mistakes', we need to try to find ways to be the rainbow in the child's storm, and not to get pulled as deeply, or as often or as quickly into the emotional quicksand or into the worry web ourselves. This is particularly important as emotions are contagious and they feed into and off each other. It is also difficult to support a child to come out of emotional quicksand, if we are also in the quicksand! Think about the

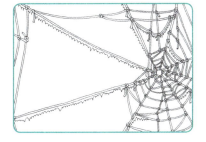

difference in how you feel when you are anxious and the other people around you are anxious (e.g. talking fast, spiralling thoughts, deep breathing, heart racing), compared to when the other people around you calmly empathise with how you are feeling, but don't add fuel, escalate, or add weight to it. As the American poet, Maya Angelou, says, 'People forget what you say, people forget what you do, but they remember how you make them feel'.

So, holding this in mind and how feelings can spread, where possible, adults need to try to guide the climate and tone for children. This is a similar notion to when a baby is crying and distressed – we know that generally one of the most effective ways to support a baby and not to escalate the situation (although it can be very trying) is to try to stay calm in our body, with our breathing, our tone of voice, our movements, and so forth. This modelling the model and setting the tone is the same with older children. Children need us, where possible, to be those safe hands, thinking minds, and regulating bodies. They need us to show them the calm, and they need to have been in repeated experiences of co-regulation (e.g. learning about recognising and responding to emotions alongside someone, within a safe relationship) with a safe adult, before they can go on to develop the sophisticated skill of self-regulation.

As parenting specialist L.R. Knost says, adults need to try to bring the calm and connection to interactions with children, rather than adding to their chaos and confusion. This can be extremely difficult, as most people operate busy lives, and have their own stressors and worries. Being on the receiving end of children's worry and anxiety can be very stressful, draining, confusing, upsetting, and frustrating. This can also be exacerbated if the surrounding adult themselves is getting triggered by the child's worries. This is one of many reasons as to why an adult's own emotional well-being, regulation skills, and self-care are so crucial and need to be supported and prioritised first (it is beyond the remit of this book to discuss this in detail here; however, interestingly, lots of the tools in this book can be useful to apply and adapt to adults).

With this in mind, if we are not able to stay calm or to model this, that is OK; it happens, it is expected, we are all only human, and no one can or is expected to do this all the time. Then we need to try to be compassionate, kind, and accepting of ourselves (as we would teach our children to be). And then, ideally, we should try to make an effort to reconnect with the child, name, own, and apologise for what happened and how we reacted, and to be aware of our responses so that we can try to do something different the next time.

Naming, labelling, empathising and labelling feelings, and teaching children about their feeling and arousal states

Coping, regulating, grounding, and calming skills and tools are not something we are born with; they are taught and learned (often over long periods of time and through lots of repetition and practice). This is through them being repeated, shown, modelled, nurtured, practised, reinforced, encouraged, and, very importantly, embodied by adults. With this in mind, it feels unfair to expect a developing and growing child to know how to express or respond to feelings of, for example, 'worry' or 'fear', or to know how to do complicated skills such as 'calming down' if they don't understand what the feeling or arousal state is, and how it feels in their mind and in their body, why it is there, what impact it has on them, and on others, and what different ways there are to respond to these big feelings. This, like coping skills, is not something we are born with; it is knowledge and feelings which we learn, and which need to be modelled and taught by our surrounding adults.

Therefore, children need to be supported by their surrounding adults to develop a rich and varied emotional dictionary, which also helps them to understand a little bit about what these feelings are, so that they have a framework and can recognise them and make sense of them. This then means that they are more able to learn ways to respond to them, as well as not getting pulled as far into a worry web, or as deep or often into the emotional quicksand. Activities throughout this book are intended to support discussions around this; however, please also see my books and cards: *A Therapeutic Treasure Box for Working with Children and Adolescents with Developmental Trauma*, *Presley the Pug Relaxation Activity Book*, and *A Therapeutic Treasure Deck of Sentence Completion and Feelings Cards* for more detailed strategies and ideas around emotional regulation.

Additionally, where possible, adults should name, be curious about, interested in, and acknowledge children's feelings and views. This is an essential part of communicating to a child that their feelings matter, are valid, important, accepted, acknowledged, encouraged, and heard. This labelling and empathising with feelings also shows children that they are entitled and safe to feel what they feel, and that these feelings can be shared, contained, accepted, and validated by other people. It also means their feelings are less likely to spill out through behaviours, or feel as overwhelming, scary, and confusing. There is nothing more powerful than someone truly feeling understood, noticed, not judged, accepted, connected with, validated, heard, and listened to by another person.

- Can you think of a time when you felt this, and how it made you feel, and the impact it had on you?

It is also helpful to remember that it can be very exposing and overwhelming for children to share their feelings, especially when they feel confused and scared by them. As shared before, it is worth holding in mind that although sometimes a situation or feeling may seem silly or trivial to you as an adult, for the child it is important, and feels big to them.

- Try to shrink yourself, and view it, or ask the child to explain it, from their size, their world, and their life experiences.

This is one of the reasons why it is important, where possible, to really listen, and to validate how difficult this can be, and to show them that you are pleased that they came to you and trusted you. It is also important to try to avoid telling children how they should feel. Their feeling is their feeling, and they are entitled to feel it.

- Put yourself in their shoes – how does it feel when someone tells you how you should feel, or dismisses how you are feeling? Or if someone tells you to stop being silly, or you share a worry, and someone tells you to stop? Does this help, or change the worry?

If you do want to explore with a child how they are feeling (some children need more scaffolding, options, and prompts than others), it can be helpful to try to do this in a curious, inquisitive, and tentative way. For example, through using statements like these:

- 'I wonder if…'
- 'If I were in that situation, I might feel…'
- 'Other people sometimes say they feel…'
- 'I am not sure, but…'
- 'When my heart is beating fast like a drum, it often is telling me… Do you think yours is telling you something similar?'
- 'I'm not surprised that you are feeling…when…'
- 'I might be wrong, and you know yourself best, but I wonder if…'

In addition, try to show that you are truly listening and trying to understand non-verbally, because matched facial expressions, nodding, open body language, eye contact, and so on can be as, if not more important, to give a child the experience of being heard. Some of the other ways we might do this labelling and validating of feelings is by saying statements such as (these can be complemented by feelings props such as feeling stamps, dolls, cards, balls, stones):

- 'Tell me if I got it wrong, but it sounds as if you feel…because…'
- 'It's so tough when you don't play football as well as you would like to. I know you tried so hard, and wanted to win. It's hard; I'm so sorry. I am here for you.'
- 'You have a right to feel that way. If it happened to me, I think I would feel the same way.'
- 'I understand that you are feeling worried. It makes sense; it's OK to feel that way. I am sorry…'
- 'Wow, that is a lot going on. I am not surprised you are feeling tangled (child's choice of word); let's think about it together.'

A catchy phrase which also supports this idea of naming, talking about, and acknowledging feelings is coined by Daniel Siegel (Siegel and Bryson 2011), who says you have to 'Name it to tame it'. This helps us to remember that often once we put a name to something, it takes some of the air out of it and makes it feel less overwhelming and less scary.

Mixed and blended feelings – and understanding the child's own experience of that feeling

Children also benefit from learning that they can have a whole range of feelings, not just positive or negative ones, but a whole mix and blend of different feelings, and that sometimes these feelings can occur at the same time, and can come in all shapes, colours, and sizes (see the introduction to Part 2 on key messages about feelings). For example, someone might feel a bit excited or feel a huge truck load of excitement, or someone might feel a bit excited about starting school, but also at the same time feel a bit worried about making new friends. This is important as, sometimes, to try to make things feel better we can overcompensate and try to emphasise the positives at the expense of validating, shutting down, and minimising the child's worries. We want them to know it is OK to have a range of feelings.

Similarly, this is where the uniqueness of the child is so key. We could have ten children who all say they feel worried, but each of those children will experience and will be meaning something different by the word 'worried' (and probably use a different word to describe worry). One child's worry might feel like a cloud over their head and be associated with the colour blue, whereas another child might feel the worry in their body like tense muscles and a beating heart. Similarly, one child might place themselves on a rating scale at a 2/10 for how worried they feel, and another at a 6/10, but this doesn't tell us much because we don't know what that number means or feels like to them, where they usually are, what they view as 'normal', where they want to be, and so on. So, it is helpful to be curious and to find out more. This is where taking a position of curiosity, exploration, and interest is so key – and appreciating that it isn't the word itself that is important, but the meaning and the rich detail within it. Activities 8–20 can support with some of this enriching and further understanding.

Mind-body links

As we know, worry and anxiety can be felt and held in our bodies. Our bodies often give us all sorts of cues, stories, signals, and signs, so it is very helpful to support children to connect with and listen to their bodies, and to link different feelings they have to their bodies. It is also helpful to teach children how to notice and differentiate these, because, for example, some sensations, like a rapid heartbeat, or butterflies in the tummy, might both be felt when a child is worried and when they are excited. There are lots of ways  we can support this connection, such as through physical movement, relaxation exercises, yoga, eating, body-mapping exercises, and so forth (examples of these are peppered throughout the story and this workbook). However, another way to support children in developing this mind-body link awareness is to verbally help them to make links between their feelings and their bodily sensations. For example:

> 'I wonder if your body could talk, what it would say…'

> 'When you say you are feeling jittery, where in your body do you notice that jittery feeling?'

> 'I wonder if you are feeling butterflies in your tummy.'

> 'I notice that your hands are tensing and you're breathing fast.'

> 'Sometimes, when I'm scared, my heart beats so fast, like a runaway train or a beating drum.'

Some children might want to extend this further and make (draw, sculpt, make, write) a visual representation of these feelings. See, for example, Activities 10–13.

Externalising and metaphors

A lot of the activities in this workbook are based around metaphors, analogies, and externalising tools. This is for numerous reasons but particularly as they can provide child-friendly and accessible ways of talking about difficulties. They can feel less threatening and overwhelming, but also helpfully can create some distance between the child and the difficulty, and can open up conversations and opportunities for play, exploration, and creativity.

One way of exploring this and expanding on these metaphors is through a technique called externalisation (most commonly associated with narrative therapy). This helps to highlight to children that the problem is the problem, not them (White 2004). It is not who they are, it doesn't define them, it is just a part or piece of them, and they are made up of loads of other parts and pieces. Externalising also allows them and the people around them some distance to be able to think about what is going on, to feel more mastery/agency over it, to feel bigger and stronger than it, and for everyone on their team to work together to solve/respond/conquer it. Activities 8–22 really play on this idea.

For example, children might like to name, describe, or externalise the worry/anxiety. They might liken it to a worry worm, a worry cloud, jiggling jelly, or a spinning wheel; everyone will find different names that resonate and fit with them. Having these names and creations can then lend themselves to child-friendly conversations around, for example, how you push the worry wall down, get unstuck from the worry web, free yourself from the worry weights, surf the worry wave, calm down the whirling tornado, and so on.

Once children have chosen and described their worry/anxiety, you might like to explore the following types of questions:

- What is... (the externalised character, object, thing of a feeling) called? What does it look like? Sound like? Smell? Say? Do?

It can also be very helpful for children to draw/paint/sculpt/mould/mosaic/depict in sand the character they create. Various questions and discussion areas can then explore the influence and impact of the worry/anxiety and also the different ways there may be to respond to it. The following list uses examples of names children have chosen for different worries. It is not an exhaustive or prescriptive list.

- How did you manage to outsmart 'Sneaky Sweats'?
- How much bigger or stronger are you than 'Dripping Derek'?
- What skills and strengths did you use to conquer 'The Whirling Worries'?
- Who would you rather have in charge of their life, 'The Worry Warts' or you?
- What is it like to share your life with 'Jittery Jared'?
- What plans does 'The Worry Waterfall' have on your life?
- What is 'The Wobbly Jelly' stopping you from doing?
- How is 'The Runaway Train' affecting your life?
- When the voice of 'The Wobbles' is less strong, what will you be doing that you're not doing now?
- How are 'The Butterflies' attempting to prevent you from...?
- What plans does 'The Jittery Jelly' have for your life?
- When 'The Worry Waterfall' is about to overflow, what do you think we can do to lessen its effect?

Providing opportunities for mastery

Often, children can feel worried, overwhelmed, and anxious when things seem out of control, and they are helpless and powerless. This is also a huge part of childhood; children primarily have other people telling them what to do, when to do it, and how to do it. While this is important, and children need structure, guidance, and scaffolding to optimally develop, and to feel safe and supported, it is also helpful to find age-appropriate ways to show the child that they can positively affect and influence change, and that their opinion is important, listened to, and valued. This includes, particularly in the context of anxiety, supporting children to recognise and practise what they can do!

Consistent and predictable parenting: rules, rituals, and routines

To increase children's sense of safety, security, containment, consistency, and predictability, and to reduce a child's anxiety, worries, and uncertainty, it is helpful for them to have a general sense of what is going to happen, what their parents/surrounding adults expect from them (sometimes this is referred to as pre-teaching) and how their carers/parents will respond to a range of situations/feelings, and what they are likely to do. Again, shrink to the child's perspective and try to imagine how it feels from their perspective, for instance, to be playing one minute, and rushing to get into the car the next.

So, for example, before going shopping, it is helpful for the adult to kindly tell the child in short, bite-size, easy-to-understand information where they are going, how long they will be there, and what they expect them to do, such as, 'I need you to walk beside the trolley holding my hand/staying close by'. Children may also need anchors, such as when we are at the till, or when we are back in the car, at the end of Peppa Pig, and so on. Phrases such as 'when...then...' can be helpful too, for example, 'When we finish the shopping, then you can have your balloon'.

Some children also benefit from having visual timetables and calendars to support them in knowing their routine, and for this to be as consistent as possible.

Having described some important underlying principles and positions, this workbook will go on to expand on various coping tools and strategies. However, first, there are some aspects to be mindful of when implementing and introducing these tools.

Some things to be mindful about some of the following strategies, including those in the child's workbook sections

- Remember to introduce these tools and techniques in a calm and containing way, and when you and the child are in a thinking and learning place. How we do it is even more important than what we do.
- We are all individual and different things work for us differently at different times. This is why having a treasure box of tools is helpful. For example, one child may find exercise releasing and re-energising, whereas for another child it might be their worst activity! Similarly, one child might find touching a material like velvet very comforting and nurturing, whereas, for another child, velvet may give them tingles up their spine and do the complete opposite!
- So, be a detective, and be curious. You know your child best, so remember to think about what will be most helpful to them as a unique individual, and feel free to be creative and adapt and make adjustments accordingly. Lots of different tools have been provided in order to give you a choice and options to narrow down – equally this is just a selection, and not an exhaustive list (most of them are included in the children's section of this workbook). The process itself of learning what works can be really useful and a great tool in itself, even more so if you make it feel like an adventure and a game!
- In line with being a detective and really noticing things, try to consider if it works, how it works, why it works, and what could make it even better. If it doesn't work, before throwing it out, think about other things that could be tweaked or tried. Sometimes, if we persist and make small changes it can make a difference. If not, then move on to the next, acknowledge and celebrate the effort, and hold on to the hope that something else will work (and remember there are loads more options).
- Once you have found something you think works, make sure you try to practise it and integrate it in a manageable and realistic way into the daily

routine, almost the same as you do with brushing teeth. The more you practise, the easier and more hardwired it becomes, and the more it goes into their muscle memory.

- Try to practise some of the tools together and/or make up your own. This not only models the model, and shows the child that you are in it together, but also gives you a flavour of the tools, makes you feel more confident about them, and can aid your own emotional well-being and self-care.
- When using sensory items, which many of the tools which follow and throughout the workbook include (particularly smelling ones), be mindful of: 1) Allergies, 2) Using age-appropriate items from a health and safety perspective, 3) Potential triggers or negative associations which some children might have to certain smells, sensations, and so on, and 4) The child's response. For example, if we are trying to support a child to relax, it is unlikely that using alerting and invigorating smells, like citrus, is going to be helpful. However, children's responses and needs will differ depending on their unique sensory profile and preferences.
- Often when using sensory tools and techniques, it is helpful to activate more than one sense to support a child to regulate and to calm down. So, for example, if a child is going into nature, all of their senses are being used naturally; however, if you are playing music, it might also be nice to also have a calming smell in the background, or for them to be looking at a calming picture, or to be drawing, at the same time, so that more than one sense and regulation system is being used to help them to feel calmer.
- Remember that for some children, you need to take a step back, and first or in parallel, prioritise the feelings vocabulary work. For example, they first need to know what calm is, and what calm feels like.
- Don't overwhelm the child or yourself – it is best to start something small and for it to be manageable, and to practise it lots and do it well before moving on to something else.
- Share with other key people, so that the team around the child are aware of the tools, and, if appropriate, are also supporting and implementing them so that it creates a consistent linked-in approach.
- Review and tweak – things change, so keep an eye on when things need to be updated again or adapted.

Coping Tools and Strategies

The majority of the ideas and tools discussed in the story and children's workbook are included and described within the children's section. So please use this section of the workbook to support them to practise these skills. However, a few additional ones, and ones which need to be expanded on, will now be described.

Talking about feeling calm and relaxed

This workbook talks a lot about helping children to learn about feeling safe, secure, calm, relaxed, and so forth. In addition to the strategies discussed above, such as modelling the model, naming it to tame it (Siegel and Bryson 2011), and trying to be the rainbow in the storm, it can also be helpful to first have age-appropriate discussions with children about what safety/calm/relaxation means to them, and to try to gain an understanding of what they think safety/relaxation/calm is, looks like, and feels like. These conversations should be fun and child-friendly, using puppets, toys, dolls, comic strips, vision boards, colours, TV or book characters, masks, and so on. Children often learn best through   fun, through play, and when conversations feel playful, don't require direct eye contact, and have a bit of distance. Activities 13, 29, and 30 might be helpful in guiding some of these discussions, but some questions you could use are outlined below. This is not a prescriptive or exhaustive list and you can replace the word 'calm' with other words such as 'safe', 'relaxed', 'peaceful', 'grounded', and so on, or even better, use the child's choice of word.

- Can you think of and describe a time when you felt really calm/when you felt really stressed? What did you notice/feel/learn?
- What does being calm mean to you? What do you think calmness feels like, sounds like, looks like?
- How would you describe feeling calm? How do you know when you are feeling calm? When do you know this?
- If the feeling of 'calmness' was an animal/item/type of weather/colour/shape, what would it be? What might it look like? What might its name be? (Children can then be supported to make, mould, sculpt, draw, or paint this.)
- What do you and others do to help you feel calm?
- What does being calm and calmness feel like or look like in your body, in your mind, on your face, and in your thoughts? Where do you feel it in your body? (Activity 13.)
- What things do you think make you feel calm? (Things you can see/hear/feel/touch/taste/smell.)

- If the feeling of 'calmness' could talk, what do you think it would say? What would its voice sound like?

These discussions about calmness/safety/relaxation can be further embedded by creating things like collages, sculptures, and posters. These can be child-led or guided, for example with the title or themes of: 'I feel calm when...', 'The things that make me feel calm are...', 'I would feel calmer if...', 'Calmness is...', 'Times that I felt calm were...'.

Using different materials, children might also like to make a calming place for a toy or an animal to be or live in.

Safe place exercise

A very helpful tool and technique can be supporting children to find a physical calming place, and also supporting them to create and bring to life their very own 'safe, happy, positive, relaxing, and soothing place/s' in their mind. In one of my other children's story and workbooks, *Presley the Pug Relaxation Activity Book*, the whole story is centred around finding a safe and calming place, so if this is a tool your child is interested in, or you think will be effective, I recommend you purchasing that workbook for far more details. However, below I will discuss how you can find and use a physical safe place, but for creating an imaginary and cognitive safe place (like an emotional safe haven, a brain break, a mind retreat, or spa), please see Activities 28–37. I also think that we all can benefit from having this type of place in our minds – I go to mine most days! So, why not create your own safe place as well – this not only helps with being the rainbow in the storm for children, but also models the model.

PHYSICAL PLACE OF SAFETY AND CALM

An actual physical place of safety should ideally be easily accessible and provide children with a sense of calm, relaxation, peace, safety, and containment. This might be a place like a local park, a quiet corner at home, a beach, or a local forest. Some homes/schools/centres will actually have an allocated place such as a sensory room, while others will have something like a thinking tent, a calm cave, a cosy corner, or a zen zone. Of course, depending on budget and space, this may need to be on a smaller scale, but there are lots of creative ways to create the same intended effect without having a designated room.

It can be helpful to support the child to have more ownership over this place, by them naming or decorating their own space. One child aptly named his safe space 'Cloud Corner', while another who used hers to reground chose 'Tree Time'. Equipment varies and ideally should be tailored to the individual child's regulation and sensory needs, preferences, and triggers, but may include things like: weighted blankets, cushions, water items, bubble machines, lava lamps, rocking chairs/rocking horse, a balancing board, a hammock, a tunnel/tube, a den/tent/tepee/mini house, a swing, massaging items, sensory boxes (see below for a step-by-step guide on making sensory and regulating boxes), beanbags, calming lighting, an aromatherapy scent kit, and soothing music (e.g. white noise, wind chimes, and/or the ocean).

Some children will naturally gravitate towards or take themselves unaided to their safe place, whereas others may need a way of communicating when they need their safe place. This might include a hand signal, a cue word, or a movement card. Others may not have the ability yet to recognise when they are dysregulated, (e.g. struggling to regulate their emotions and arousal) so the surrounding adults will need to actively support them around this, and gently remind and guide them.

As with all new strategies, the safe space should be introduced to the child when they are in a thinking, learning, and regulated place. Following this, and while in a thinking space, children should have a few turns at practising and role-playing how and when to use their safe space. Some children might prefer to practise and/or role-play putting their favourite toy into the safe space before they have a go themselves. These times and ideas can then be strengthened by writing them down, drawing them, sculpting them, representing them in sand, creating a social story, or making a reminder poster, for example 'Times when I can use my safe place' or 'My safe place makes me feel…'. The safe space should be emphasised as a safe positive space, and not used as a place of punishment or exclusion.

Creating a soothing and calming box

This will offer you some explanation and step-by-step instructions, but see Activity 38 for all the supporting information and worksheet.

A soothing box can be called many things: a safe box, happy box, calming box, sensory box – or even better, the child can choose their own special name for it that fits for them. It can support a child to actively learn and develop different self-soothing, grounding, self-nurturing, self-regulating, and coping strategies to support their internal and external sense of safety.

It is a fun, creative, and multi-sensory activity that stimulates and draws on all of the five senses and can help children to create a calming mood. This, alongside other strategies, can engage lots of the child's regulation, emotional, and arousal systems, can soothe the lower parts of their brain, and activate their body's relaxation and stress reduction

responses. Additionally, this box can act as a physical container and transitional object. As it is created positively within a relationship, it therefore has relational elements (e.g. co-regulation) which can be internalised and anchored on to by the child in times of distress. It also gives the child something tangible which they can see, practise, and do – it is a physical way of organising and putting lots of other strategies in one place. For example, a child can put their favourite relaxation prompt cards in it, or add a sensory bottle to it.

Here are some simple steps to follow when introducing the box:

1. Discuss the rationale of the box in a child-friendly way. Find out if it is something that the child thinks may be helpful and is open to trying. The more they are involved and invested in the process, the better.
2. Find a shoebox or container that will form the basis of the box. If the child prefers to use a different form of container, that's fine too – ideally, they will choose all the elements – but try to ensure that it is big enough for the intended contents and will be durable.
3. Start a conversation about things that make the child feel calm, relaxed, nurtured, safe, happy, and warm. Questions might range from their favourite season of the year, to their best meal, to their biggest role model, to their favourite song. Try to incorporate a range of questions that include enquiring about all of their senses. If the child brings up negative images, acknowledge these, validate them, discuss them, and memory bank them (save them for later) for other future tasks.
4. Encourage the child to decorate and name the container. Make sure you have glue and scissors, as the majority of children like to decorate their boxes with additional materials, such as stickers, soothing fabrics, tissue paper, photographs, textured paper and wrap, and glitter.
5. Help the child to collect a range of images or objects to represent the things that make them feel calm, relaxed, and nurtured. Ideally, many of the items will also match the child's responses to the questions about the things that make them feel happy and calm. For example, a child who says their favourite time of year is winter and when it snows may be supported to have or make a snow globe, as well as pictures of snow, or maybe some snowflake art. Similarly, a child who likes stroking fluffy dogs may be supported to buy or have some fluffy material resembling the hair of a fluffy dog, or have a little dog toy, or some photos of a dog.
6. If an adult has collected the images, make sure the child has the opportunity to choose which ones they want. Consider saving several copies of the images, in case the originals are lost or damaged. The child/adult can cut them up and incorporate them into other activities, such as in their safe-place poster, or add them to the contents of the box.
7. Objects can then be placed into the sensory calming box. Some children may find lots of objects helpful; others might find this overwhelming and too much, so might find it more helpful to focus on a small collection of items.
8. When in their 'thinking brain' and a regulated place (e.g. settled, calm, open, present), the child should be encouraged to practise using the items in the box. Items and their usefulness should be explored and evaluated by both the child and the person supporting them to make the box. The child should also be supported in thinking about a range of different scenarios/situations/feeling states where the box may or may not be helpful.
9. Encourage the child to use their box during the day and before bed, as part of their winding-down and relaxation routine. The more they practise this, the more it will become part of their muscle memory and will be easier to

access in times when they need it. Also, it is better to use it as a preventative measure and something to avoid escalation, than using it in the midst of a big emotion! Children might also benefit from having a mini version of their box or a duplicate they can have with them at school, in the car, and so on.

See Activity 38 for a list of some common items that children include. Try to consider experiences which will help to calm the different senses.

As an alternative, using similar concepts, a child may prefer to make a sensory tray, a sensory board, a sensory book, or sensory/mindful/calming bottles or jars (such as a glitter bottle).

What is working well? Reviewing and measuring progress, as well as keeping a record

Once you have gone through this workbook and tried a range of different ideas and tools, it is important to review and evaluate them. Encourage children (and try to encourage yourself!) to be like a detective: analyse what works, and then consider why and how it works. It might be as simple as having a conversation with your child and asking them outright or observing what happens when you try different approaches. Be curious and think about keeping a shared diary or a chart to record any changes. Encourage the child to think about their feelings, thoughts, behaviours, and body sensations before and after the activities.

Then, once you have found your top ones (these might change and need to be adjusted and added to), try to keep a record of these things. This way, the child has a reminder of all of the things that they can actively do and feels that they have an array of options and tricks to try, and some agency and control over the situation. This also teaches the child the importance of having coping tools to use that can potentially travel with them through all their different situations and life stages. As ever, have fun with different ways to record these ideas and tailor them to the child's interests. Some ideas include:

- a train of coping tools, with each carriage representing a different tool
- an octopus of options, with each tentacle showing a different coping option or a different helpful person (as in the photo)
- a protective palm, with each helpful tool on the fingers and thumb (as in the photo)
- a calm-down superhero, with tools written on a cape or on a superhero figure
- a treasure box of tools and tricks (see Activity 51)
- a wizard hat and wand of tools (see Activity 52)
- a tower of tricks and tools.

I hope you have found this workbook helpful and fun, and I wish you luck and success in your quest to find calm.

References and Further Reading

Siegel, D.J. and Bryson, T.P. (2011) *The Whole-Brain Child: 12 Revolutionary Strategies to Nurture Your Child's Developing Mind.* New York, NY: Delacorte Press.

Treisman, K. (2017) *A Therapeutic Treasure Box for Working with Children and Adolescents with Developmental Trauma: Creative Techniques and Activities.* London: Jessica Kingsley Publishers.

Treisman, K. (2017) *A Therapeutic Treasure Deck of Sentence Completion and Feelings Cards.* London: Jessica Kingsley Publishers.

Treisman, K. (2017) *A Therapeutic Treasure Deck of Grounding, Soothing, Coping and Regulating Cards.* London: Jessica Kingsley Publishers.

Treisman, K. (2018) *Neon the Nightmare Ninja Activity Book for Children Who Struggle with Sleep and Nightmares: A Therapeutic Story with Creative Activities for Children Aged 5–10.* London: Jessica Kingsley Publishers.

Treisman, K. (2018) *Presley the Pug Relaxation Activity Book: A Therapeutic Story with Creative Activities about Finding Calm for Children Aged 5–10 Who Worry.* London: Jessica Kingsley Publishers.

Treisman, K. (2018) *Gilly the Giraffe Self-Esteem Activity Book: A Therapeutic Story with Creative Activities for Children Aged 5–10.* London: Jessica Kingsley Publishers.

White, M. (2004) 'Working with people who are suffering the consequences of multiple trauma: A narrative perspective.' *The International Journal of Narrative Therapy and Community Work* 1, 45–76.

Popular apps for supporting children to relax

This is by no means an exhaustive or prescriptive list:

- The dreamy kid.
- Stop, breathe, and think.
- Breathe, think, do Sesame.
- Breathing bubbles.
- Smiling minds.
- Chill outz.
- Super stretch yoga.
- Relax melodies.
- Calming bottle.
- Calm counter.
- Kids yoga deck.

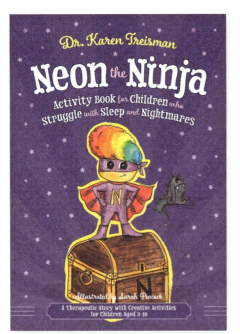

Neon the Ninja Activity Book for Children who Struggle with Sleep and Nightmares

A Therapeutic Story with Creative Activities for Children Aged 5–10

Dr. Karen Treisman

£18.99 | $26.95 | 128PP | PAPERBACK | ISBN: 978 1 78592 550 4 | EISBN: 978 1 78775 002 9

Neon the Ninja has a very special job. He looks after anyone who finds the night time scary. Lots of us have nightmares, but Neon loves nothing more than using his special ninja powers to keep the nightmares and worries far away, and to keep the magical dreams and positive thoughts close by.

It combines a fun illustrated story to show children how Neon the Ninja can reduce their nightmares and night worries with fun activities and therapeutic worksheets to make night times feel safer and more relaxed. This workbook contains a treasure trove of explanations, advice, and practical strategies for parents, carers and professionals. Based on creative, narrative, sensory, and CBT techniques, it is full of tried and tested exercises, tips and techniques to aid and alleviate nightmares and sleeping difficulties. This is a must-have for those working and living with children aged 5–10 who experience nightmares or other sleep-related problems.

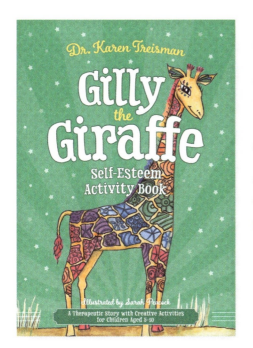

Gilly the Giraffe Self-Esteem Activity Book

A Therapeutic Story with Creative Activities for Children Aged 5–10

Dr. Karen Treisman

£18.99 | $26.95 | 144PP | PAPERBACK | ISBN: 978 1 78592 552 8 | EISBN: 978 1 78775 003 6

Even though Gilly the Giraffe has many wonderful things in her life, she sometimes lacks confidence. Why does she have to stand out so much with her long neck, her long black tongue and her mosaic patches? Why do some of the other animals point and laugh at her? Can it be possible to be different and to be cool?

This activity book developed by expert child psychologist Dr. Karen Treisman combines a colourfully illustrated therapeutic story about Gilly the Giraffe to help start conversations, which is followed by a wealth of creative activities for children to explore and build upon some of the ideas raised in the story, and beyond!

The activities are accompanied by extensive advice and practical strategies for parents, carers and professionals on how to help children aged 5–10 boost their self-esteem and confidence.

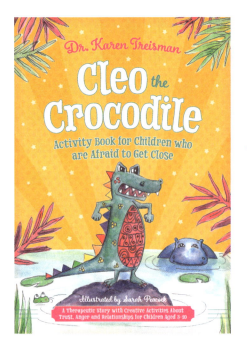

Cleo the Crocodile Activity Book for Children who are Afraid to Get Close

A Therapeutic Story with Creative Activities About Trust, Anger and Relationships for Children Aged 5–10

Dr. Karen Treisman

£18.99 | $26.95 | 160PP | PAPERBACK | ISBN: 978 1 78592 551 1 | EISBN: 978 1 78775 078 4

Amongst the beauty of the Okavango delta in Botswana, Cleo the Crocodile loved having fun with all of his animal friends. That is, until one day Hogan the Hippo, who was supposed to look after Cleo, started to act mean and hurt him. Cleo has to leave the swamp to find a safe new home - he's scared and puts his prickles up for protection, so all the other animals are afraid of him. How can Cleo find a new safe home? How can he make new friends when he doesn't know who he can trust?

This activity book developed by expert child psychologist Dr. Karen Treisman combines a colourfully illustrated therapeutic story about Cleo the Crocodile to help start and enrich conversations, which is followed by a wealth of creative activities and photocopiable worksheets for children to explore issues relating to attachment, relationships, rejection, anger, trust and much more.

The activities are accompanied by extensive advice and practical strategies for parents, carers, and professionals on how to help children aged 5-10 to start to name their tricky feelings. It will help children to understand their own prickles, to trust others and begin to invest in relationships so they can let others close again.

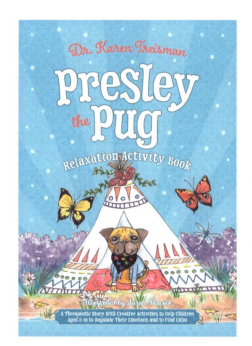

Presley the Pug Relaxation Activity Book

A Therapeutic Story With Creative Activities to Help Children Aged 5–10 to Regulate Their Emotions and to Find Calm

Dr. Karen Treisman

£18.99 | $26.95 | 144PP | PAPERBACK | ISBN: 978 1 78592 553 5 | EISBN: 978 1 78775 110 1

Like all dogs, Presley the Pug loves to play, run, and snuggle up under his warm blanket. But sometimes, Presley gets gets so excited that his feelings take over.

Sometimes it's anger, sometimes stress, sometimes worry. He doesn't know how to calm down! What can Presley do when he feels like this? Luckily Presley's canine friends are nearby with some wise words and they share some of the tricks that have worked for them!

This therapeutic activity book was developed by expert child psychologist Dr Karen Treisman. It features a colourful therapeutic story designed to help start conversations about coping with big feelings and how to find calm. It explains how Presley (and the reader!) is able to create a 'mind retreat' - an imaginary safe space where he can relax.

The activity book is also packed with creative activities and photocopiable worksheets to help children to explore the ideas raised in the story, including regulating and coping tools like sensory boxes, relaxation exercises and easy yoga poses. It also features advice and practical strategies for parents, carers and professionals supporting children aged 5–10.

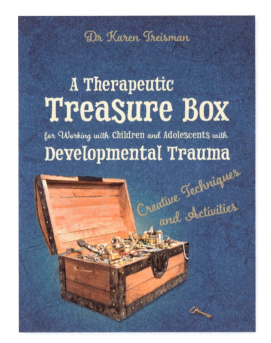

A Therapeutic Treasure Box for Working with Children and Adolescents with Developmental Trauma

Creative Techniques and Activities

Dr. Karen Treisman

£29.99 | $39.95 | 424PP | PAPERBACK | ISBN: 978 1 78592 263 3 | EISBN: 978 1 78450 553 0

Like a treasure chest, this resource overflows with valuable resources – information, ideas and techniques to inspire and support those working with children who have experienced relational and developmental trauma.

Drawing on a range of therapeutic models including systemic, psychodynamic, trauma, sensory, neurobiological, neurocognitive, attachment, cognitive behavioural, and creative ideas, Dr. Karen Treisman explains how we understand trauma and its impact on children, teens, and their families. She details how it can be seen in symptoms such as nightmares, sleeping difficulties, emotional dysregulation, rage, and outbursts.

Theory and strategies are accompanied by a treasure trove of practical, creative, and ready-to-use resources including over 100 illustrated worksheets and handouts, top tips, recommended sample questions, and photographed examples.

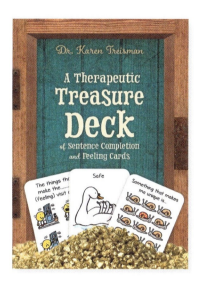

A Therapeutic Treasure Deck of Sentence Completion and Feelings Cards
Dr. Karen Treisman

£22.99 | $29.95 | CARD SET | ISBN: 978 1 78592 398 2

The perfect tool to add to any 'therapeutic treasure box', this set of 68 cards provide a way to help open conversations and structure discussions with children and adolescents aged 6+.

The treasure deck offers a fun, non-threatening way to help to build understanding and forge relationships. It also provides a safe, playful way for children to articulate and make sense of their feelings, thoughts, experiences and beliefs. The deck comes with two different types of card – the 'feelings cards' and the 'sentence-completion cards' – which can be used separately or together, and the cards are accompanied by a booklet which explains some of the different ways in which they can be therapeutically used.

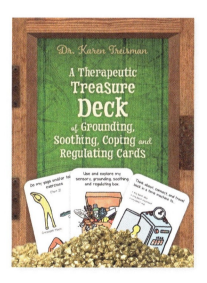

A Therapeutic Treasure Deck of Grounding, Soothing, Coping and Regulating Cards
Dr. Karen Treisman

£22.99 | $32.95 |CARD SET | ISBN: 978 1 78592 529 0

A treasure trove of coping, regulating, grounding, and soothing activities and techniques for working with children (aged 6+), teens and adults.

This pack of 70 cards and explanatory guide offers a playful, non-threatening way to explore feelings, and to form effective coping, regulating, soothing, and grounding strategies through a range of games and activities. Designed to work with both the brain and body, the cards address a wide range of common issues including anxiety, stress, low mood, sleep difficulties and emotional dysregulation. To do so, they employ a range of proven strategies including cognitive techniques, nurturing activities, sensory strategies, body-based activity and creative exercises.